She Got it Bad for A Springfield Hitta:

Sen & Skylen's Story

Tisha Monet

© **2018**
Published by *Miss Candice Presents*

IISHA MONET

Sen

"Ooooh yessss, eat this pussy just like that. Just like thatttttt." Ol girl moaned as I silently watched some fat cornball ass nigga eat her pussy unaware of his surroundings.

Twisting on my silencer, I slowly made my way into the room and pointed my gun at both of them, and the girl screamed alarming whoever the fuck this clown ass nigga was in between her legs. Turning around and facing me he screwed up his face before he began talkin' shit.

"You know who the fuck I am muthafucka?" He asked me with some bass in his voice making me chuckle a bit.

To be honest, I didn't give a fuck about who he was, but like always I did my research. Nigga was the head nigga in charge on this side of town but I didn't give a fuck. I was here for one thing and one thing only. Money. Out the corner of my eye, I saw shorty reach for somethin'.

"I wouldn't do that if I was you," I warned her in a calm tone never taking my eyes off of my target.

"Open the safe!"

"Nigga I ain't opening shi-" he tried to bark before I let off a shot hitting him in the shoulder.

"Open the fuckin' safe. I know you got one around this muthafucka!"

"Ahhhhh! Fuck man! You really gon' do this wit' my ol' lady sittin' here?!"

"Unless you want her pretty little face blown the fuck off you'll stop the small talk and lead me to where the fuck I need to be. Choice is yours."

"Baby please just show him where it's at!" His bitch cried irritating the fuck outta me.

After a few minutes of us staring at one another, he finally agreed to take me to his safe. Even if he hadn't, I was goin' to get what the fuck I came here for, kill his ass and dip. Either way, a nigga wasn't leaving this bitch empty-handed.

Instructing him to get up with my gun still pointed at his head, he led the way to his safe. Once we were there, he entered the code, and it opened.

"Nothing personal bruh, just business," I said nonchalantly as he turned around and I fired a shot hitting him between his eyes killing him instantly, just as shorty came and stood next to me.

"I thought you said we weren't killing anyone today Sen! You said we weren't going to kill him!" She said with agitation in her voice.

"I know what the fuck I said but what sense would it make to let the fat ma'fucka live? Grab the money and let's go!" I barked at Valencia before turning and walking away wiping the place down getting rid of any fingerprints that her dumb ass may have left.

Once we cleaned house, it was time for us to get the fuck up out of there. I never stayed at a job longer than I had to. With this robbin' shit, you had to be in and out, or shit could go wrong very fuckin' fast.

My fault man, I didn't even introduce myself. The name is Sen. As you may have already figured out

I rob muthafuckas for a living and made great money doing so with my girl by my side. Speaking on her, Valencia set me up with my very first lick a couple of years ago while we was out in Brooklyn. Shorty was partying with some girls she used to strip with, and at the time I was doing some bullshit ass hustling.

Long story short, nigga wanted her to go home with him. She, of course, turned him down but the nigga started flashing his money, and she agreed. Sent me a text once she was at his crib and told me he had had money laying around on some dumb shit and to come through. So I did and we been hittin' licks together ever since.

"How much you think we got?" she asked me as she drove away.

"I don't know. But judging by how neatly shit was wrapped I'd say about fifteen bands or so." I responded to her before getting quiet again.

I was a beast at this shit. Never have we gotten caught or even gotten close to it, but lately it's been feelin' like maybe my luck was runnin' out. I can't explain it, but somethin' wasn't feelin' right. It could very well just be me being paranoid, but I know this shit ain't going last forever. Not to mention Valencia.

Valencia and I been rockin' for about five years now and out of those five we've been doing this shit for about two. Every lick required her to get involved with the target and every time ended with me murkin' a ma'fucka. But this time she seemed different as if she was feelin' the nigga.

You saw how she got mad as soon as the bullet pierced his skull. Shorty had a whole attitude. Not to mention when he was eatin' her pussy she was enjoying it a little too much for my fuckin' liking. I wasn't wit' it. He risked his life to save hers, and that alone let me know that there was more to them besides him being a mark for us.

I never been too comfortable with niggas touchin', rubbin' and kissin' all on my girl, but I dealt wit' it because she always looked at it as a job but tonight? Tonight, I saw something different in her eyes. I saw hurt. I think I even saw love. Crazy shit, huh?

****

"What's good fam?" I dapped up my nigga Grimey takin a seat across from him.

"Ain't shit. Coolin'. Sup wit you nigga?" He asked smokin' a blunt.

"Shit. You know me. Just stayin' out the way and gettin' this money. Tryna stay above ground, feel me?"

"Heard you. You need to get in on this pill shit wit' me. Mad money out here. Bitches buying these shits left and right."

"You know that ain't me. Too risky. You fuckin' wit' the doctors and shit. As soon as they ass is jammed up they tellin everything. I can't afford to take that kind of loss."

"So hittin' licks ain't risky nigga?" He asked sarcastically, and I shrugged my shoulders before responding.

"Shit it is, but I know what the fuck I'm getting myself into. I know the protocols to take."

"I hear you. I'm just sayin' you may want to switch it up. You can never have too many hustles. You living good and shit but why not live better?"

"Fuck is you? My financial advisor?"

"Nah man. I'm just lookin' out for my bro. That's all."

"Preciate it."

"What's the word for tonight? We hittin' Center?" He asked me referring to the strip club Center Stage.

"I'm wit' it. I'm bringing Valenicia though, that's cool?"

"Nigga we ain't goin' there on business."

"It's always business. It's the weekend too. Them CT niggas gon' be out here. Ain't shit wrong with a quick lick." I expressed, and he nodded his head in agreement.

I wasn't big on goin' out. I never understood the point of spending money to get into a place to not enjoy yourself. Shit didn't make sense. And to be honest with you I didn't drink. I can have a beer and be straight but other than that drinking has never been my thing. Neither has smoking. I just wasn't that kind of nigga.

So you see if a nigga was about to spend some bread to go out tonight, I was going to make sure to bring my baddest accessory with me. Baby is a real head turner and tonight just might be a lucky night.

Skylen

"You about to take your break?" my coworker and friend Lauren asked me as I got up from my desk.

"Yeah, you coming with?"

"You going out to get lunch?"

"Yeah. I think I'm going to grab something quick from Burger King." I told her preparing to walk away.

"Okay, give me a sec. I'm coming!"

"Meet me at my car. I'll be waiting."

"K!" She said, and I walked away.

I was so ready to clock out of work. These eight hours weren't coming to an end fast enough. Working at a call center was something I wasn't proud of. The pay was cool, but the cattiness amongst all the women is what made it drag. I wasn't a mean person on any level, but when it came to my coworkers, I couldn't stand these bitches.

Getting inside of my car, I started my ignition and called my boyfriend, Leland. Leland and I have been together since high school, so I guess you could call us high school sweethearts. He was the captain of the basketball team, and I was the cheerleader girlfriend. Sounds like a fairytale, right? Boy meets girl, they fall in love, and everything is rose petals and candles. Not our case. We've been through our share of things but he was my baby, and at twenty-six I couldn't imagine leaving him and starting over with someone else.

"Who this?" He asked answering the phone causing me to kiss my teeth and roll my eyes.

"Who you think?" I asked him with an attitude.

"Oh, my bad bae, wassup? You good?"

"Yeah, I'm good. What you doing?"

"Shit, playin' this new 2k. What you doing?"

"I'm at work. You know the place you have to clock into in order to live. The place you need to be at." I replied irritated.

I was so sick of him laying around doing absolutely nothing while I busted my ass day in and day out at a job I hated.

"Mannnn don't nobody want to hear that shit! I told you I've been lookin'!"

"Clearly you aren't lookin' hard enough. It's been three years Leland! Three fuckin' years and I'm tired of this shit."

"Why you always naggin' me? A nigga gets tired of hearing you complain all the time!" He had the nerve to say making me look at my phone to see if I was indeed talking to his unemployed ass.

"Nigga is you-"

"Bye Skylen!"

"Don't you hang up on me!" I yelled into the phone all for him to hang up on me. Before I got a chance to call him back Lauren was opening my passenger car door.

Getting into the car, she put her seatbelt on before looking at me. I couldn't look at her. Everything in me wanted to cry but I couldn't. At least not in front of Lauren. I was so tired of living like this.

I was tired of taking care of a grown ass man. I was tired of it all, but I had no room to complain as long as I continued to deal with it. I loved him so much that life without him didn't even seem right. We've known each other forever, and he's the only man I have ever been with. So as you see, I was too invested in this relationship. Although I was tired of being in this relationship I also wasn't sure if I wanted to know what it would be like without him.

"You okay?" Lauren asked me in a soft voice. She knew something was wrong with me. She always knew.

"Yeah, I'm okay. Ready?" I spoke to her not looking at her.

"Sky."

"Not now Laur. Not now."

"Okay. Just know I'm here if you need me."

"I know you are. Thank you."

"Sooooo, I was thinking and now is the perfect time."

"Thinking about?"

"We haven't gone out in a long time. We're due for a ladies night!" She beamed, and I let out a frustrated breath.

"Can't. You know I don't have any money to go out with." I replied back to her as I continued driving.

"Skylennnnn, come onnnnn!"

"I just told you I was broke."

"It'll be my treat! Come on, live a little!"

"Laur. what the fuck am I supposed to wear?"

"Clothes hoe! I know you have some clothes in your closet. We can do dinner and then go out. That way you know who won't ask too many questions," she suggested. It sounded good, but I wasn't the partying type. I was a homebody.

"I don't know. You know when I go home I'll probably take a nap, and you know once I wake up-"

"I'm not taking no for an answer! You're getting out tonight, and that's final! I'm picking you up at nine, so your ass better be ready!"

"Did I ever tell you how much I didn't like you?"

"The devil is a lie! You loooovvveeee me!" She teased sticking her tongue out.

Now I have to figure out what I have in my closet now. I silently thought to myself pulling up to Burger King.

***

Moving around Leland and I small one-bedroom apartment, I was back and forth from the bathroom and our bedroom as he stared a hole into me. I was purposely ignoring any eye contact with him. I only knew he was looking at me because I could feel him doing so. If he had it his way, I would stay home all day long and just cater to him. He had some serious mommy issues.

Stepping into the tight-fitting black bodycon dress, I pulled it up and adjusted my titties so that they were sitting up nice and perky. Feeling myself a little a did a cute little spin before blowing myself a kiss in the - full-length mirror. I was impressed with my look. I had my hair in a high ponytail, a nice simple face with a bold matte red lipstick making my lips appear very plumped.

"Where you think you going?" He asked standing behind me while I continued to look at myself in awe.

"Out."

"That ain't a place."

"I'm going to dinner. Any more questions?" I asked him locking eyes with him in the mirror.

"I never told you, you could go."

"I didn't know I needed your permission."

"You don't think you should have asked me whether or not I would be cool with you going out?"

"You're joking, right?" I asked rolling my eyes.

"Does it look like I'm joking to you?"

"Get over yourself Leland. It ain't that serious. I'm going to dinner with Lauren whether you like it or not."

"Well, I need the car tonight."

"And?" I questioned just as my cell phone chimed and I moved away from him and grabbed it from the charger. It was Lauren letting me know she was outside.

"I'm gone," I told him grabbing my clutch and walking out of our bedroom.

I wasn't going to let him ruin my night. I looked and felt good, and for the first time in a while, I was going to enjoy myself.

Sen

"So, are we going out tonight as business or pleasure?" Valencia asked me strapping her black heels on.

"Pleasure but you know I'm always working. You know what to do if you see a potential target." I spoke leaning on the door frame as I admired her beauty.

"I know baby. Just don't make shit hot."

"Make shit hot? Fuck is that supposed to mean?"

"You know. like stand there staring at people like a weirdo."

"I'm just an observant nigga."

"You call it being observant, and others would say that you have a serious eye problem. If I manage to find someone just fall back and let me do my thing. We've done this a thousand times. I know what to do."

"Aight. You got it. Say less. I'll wait for you outside." I told her and walked away calling Grimey.

"Yooooooo!" He yelled answering the phone.

"Fuck is you up to goofy?"

"Shit, blowin back some kush. You still coming out tonight?"

"Yeah. Time you was thinkin' bout heading out?" I asked checking the time on my Salvatore Ferragamo Feroni Bracelet watch.

"I'll probably head downtown in about twenty. Got a play to make and then I'm on my way."

"Aight. Bet. See you there."

"Aye, you really bringing Valencia?" He asked before I had a chance to disconnect our call.

"Yeah nigga, why?"

"Can't take a day off huh?"

"No such thing as a day off. I'll see you though." I told him and hung up just as shorty came strutting out of our house.

"You look nice." I complimented her once she got close enough to me.

"Thank you, baby. You don't look bad yourself." She flirted, and I brought her lips to mine kissing her.

"Mmmmm, don't start nothing and you can't finish."

"Is that right?"

"Yupp. If you ain't tryna slide your dick in my tight wet walls, then don't start nothing."

"You testing me?"

"Never. But I know when you have your mind set on something, you have tunnel vision."

"You think you know me?" I asked in a raspy voice palming her ass.

"I do. Let's go." She smiled before wiggling out of my hold and getting into her 2016 Honda Accord.

****

You know you the baddest baby, fuck them hoes. Fuck them hoes, fuck them

hoes. We on a different planet girl it's fuck them hoes. Fuck them hoes, fuck them hoes.

Grimey and I walked into the strip club being sure to walk a few feet from Valencia. Taking my eyes away from her I turned my attention to some thick brown skin girl who was dancing to the future track that was playing. Shorty was stacked, but her face wasn't all that. She had the niggas enticed though, to say the least. It was still kinda early, but this bitch was flooded.

Finding a corner, I stood off in the shadows as I watched Grimey dap up a few niggas while Valencia hugged some girl I have never even seen before; all while some flashy ma'fucka walked up to them trying to get her attention. It worked because seconds later she had managed to walk with him to the bar with a smile plastered on her face.

Sometimes I wondered if she got a kick out of this. She knew she was irresistible and most of the niggas we ran licks on wouldn't have the time of day with her if it wasn't for business. She was shallow. I mean I wasn't the finest nigga in the field, but a nigga wasn't the ugliest, feel me?

Like I stated before when I met her I was hustlin' weed. Nothing major. I was gettin' money but not the way I was gettin it now. The type of bitch Cia was she wasn't fuckin' with a nigga who wasn't out here gettin' to that bag. In my opinion, money has always been the motive for her.

"I can't believe this bitch brought me to a fuckin' strip club." Some random girl spoke to herself standing next to me.

"You talkin' to yourself ma?" I asked her, and her face dropped in embarrassment.

"Did I say that out loud? I thought I was thinking to myself. My bad."

"No need to apologize. You good."

"Nah, I don't want you thinking I'm a crazy person. I don't normally do that." She said with a light giggle.

"Trust me. You good. My old lady says as long as you ain't answerin' yourself back you shouldn't worry." I told her with a smirk before the girl I'm assuming was Lauren came over to her grabbing her hand and they walked away leaving me alone again to keep my eye on Valencia.

That didn't last long though because shortly after Grimey walked up to me with a couple of bitches. Shit like this is why I didn't go out with this nigga. My girl is feet away and he on some other shit. I didn't have time for this.

Valencia

"So where's your nigga at? I know a girl as fine as you gotta have a nigga tucked off somewhere." The guy Tee spoke into my ear.

"I'm single," I stated seductively before glancing over at Sen. Him, and Grimey had a gang of bitches posted around them and I instantly felt my blood boil.

Here I was setting niggas up for him and he in here entertaining thot ass bitches. Granted he probably didn't invite them, bitches, to be in his face, but he was still ke-keing like I wasn't in here with him. When we get home tonight, I was cutting into his ass something serious.

"You gon' answer me or what?" I heard dude say snapping me out of my thoughts.

"What did you say?"

"Word? You ain't even listening to a nigga?"

"It's not like that. I thought I saw my little sister

in here and I was trying to see if it was her or not." I lied.

"I'm sorry."

"It's cool. You want to just take down my number or somethin'?"

"Yeah, let's do that."

"Aight bet." He spoke before giving me his number. Making sure to save it I told him I'd be in contact soon before making my way to the bathroom being sure to roll my eyes at Sen in the process. *Black bastard.* I thought as he looked at me confused.

Once I got in the bathroom, I went into one of the stalls and pulled out a lil sack of coke. I know what you're thinking, but it ain't like that. I only sniff when I'm out partying or when I go out with the mark. It helps keep me numb. When I'm sober, I think about any and everything.

Taking the little small compact mirror, I put a perfect line on it before rollin' up a dollar bill and inhaling my favorite drug of choice before pinching my nose and tilting my head back allowing the high to consume me. After a few more lines, I walked out of the stall and stood in front of the full-length mirror making sure to get rid of any white residue that was left over.

Giving myself a once over I grabbed my things turning to prepare myself to walk out as soon as the door swung open startling me. Seeing two girls walk in I quickly noticed that I knew the brown skin girl.

"Skylen?" I questioned.

"Valencia, right?" She asked, and I nodded my head yes.

"How have you been? I haven't seen you since middle school!"

"Damn it's been that long?"

"I know right. Feel like we were just in Social Studies acting a damn fool in Mr. Stacey's class."

"Oh, My God! I know he was glad when school was over for us. We got on his nervessss!"

"He was a bit off anyway. I swear something

was wrong with him." She giggled.

"So what's new? Married? Any kids?"

"Not married, I have a boyfriend. One child. She's twelve," I replied to her.

Yes, you heard right. I have a twelve-year-old daughter that slid out of my pussy. I got pregnant young. Literally the first time I ever had sex I ended up knocked up. Ain't that a bitch? I wasn't ready to be a mother, so I gave her to my mother and long story short I never went back for her. Irresponsible but I don't give a fuck. I wasn't ready to be nobody's damn mamma!

"Oh Wow. Congratulations!"

"Thanks, girl. Wassup with you?"

"Nothing. No kids. I have a boyfriend though."

"And y'all don't have any kids?" I asked not really caring.

"No. I don't think we're ready for kids to be honest."

"Well, I'm sure when the two of you are ready you'll have a baby of your own."

"Maybe you're right." She spoke just as the girl who was with her cleared her throat.

"Oh, I'm sorry. Valencia meet Lauren. Lauren meet Valencia."

"Hi." The chick Lauren greeted all dry which was fine because I wasn't going to speak to her basic ass.

"Well, I gotta get back out there. My boyfriend is waiting on me. Maybe we can do lunch or something?" I asked genuinely. I didn't have friends, but Skylen was one of my closest friends in middle school when we were going to Kiley. I wouldn't mind seeing her again.

"Sure, take my number."

Pulling out my phone I entered her phone number before walking out of the bathroom. Tee the guy I was talking to was now in a whole different bitch face while Sen was still in the corner. I'm secretly hoping the Tee dude calls me. For obvious reasons of course, but I saw his print, and I wanted to sample. The way he carries himself all cocky like has me wondering if the nigga was a beast in the sheets and I have every intention on finding out.

Walking up to Sen I let him know that I was ready to go and judging by his face he couldn't wait to get up out of here. Him and Grimey aggy ass exchanged a few words before him, and I walked out and went to the car. As soon as we got in there, I cut into his ass.

"So you like having bitches all in your face?"

"Fuck is you talking about?" he questioned annoyed.

"You heard me. You like having bitches all in your face?"

"You have niggas all in your face every day, and I don't say shit."

"That's different. Those niggas usually turn into targets stupid! You was all laughing and shit with a group of bitches. What the fuck is funny in the muthafuckin strip club?" I asked rolling my eyes.

"You trippin' trippin'."

"Nah, you are. Don't be disrespecting me when we're out."

"You finished or is you done?"

"Don't try to be funny Sen!"

"I ain't hearing none of the bullshit you talkin'. Grimey brought them hoes over. I didn't exchange numbers with them, so you trippin' for nothing. You worried about bitches that ain't worried about you or me."

"Yeah, whatever."

"How your little meet and greet go?" He asked talking about the dude from the strip club.

"Cool. He said he's going to call me." I said before turning up the radio.

This shit was getting old fast.

Skylen

"Thank you, Laur. I really needed this night out." I confessed smiling while we sat in front of my apartment in her car.

"No problem boo. You know I'm always here to save the day!" She joked.

"Save the day, huh?"

"Yeah, girl. All you do is sit in the house. You're twenty-six you need to get out more. Leland ain't going nowhere."

"Lauren, can I tell you something?"

"You know you can. Wassup boo?" She asked me.

"I want to leave Leland." I blurted out, and she looked at me with a crazy expression on her face.

"I just can't deal with him anymore. Do you know the nigga tried telling me I couldn't leave to go out tonight? I go to work five days sometimes six days a week to pay our rent and bills, and he had the nerve to try to tell me that I couldn't leave. Me! The fucking breadwinner in the relationship. I swear ever since he lost his scholarship from UMASS he's been different."

"Well, I'm glad you didn't let him win and stay home. You deserve a night out every so often. You also deserve a man and not a boy. He has some growing to do. Leland is still attached to his momma's titty!" she expressed angrily just as a car pulled up behind us and I quickly recognized it as mine.

Instead of getting out of Lauren's car I watched him get out of the car and stumble to our door. Not only did he take my car he also was driving drunk, like that shit wasn't illegal. Not to mention where the hell did his broke ass manage to get money from to drink? See why I was tired of this relationship? This is what things have been like for the past three years.

I understand that he went through shit with school, but at the same time, he needed to get the fuck over it. He was too grown to be carrying on the way that he has been. Seriously it was beginning to get old.

"Let me go in this house girl. Call or text me and let me know that you made it home safely." I told her getting out of her car.

"Sky, you deserve to be happy. Tonight, was the first time I have ever seen you smile a real smile in a while. Don't let him take that from you." Lauren said out of her window before pulling off.

Walking up the walkway that led to our apartment I took a couple of deep breaths before going inside. Removing my heels at the door, I went straight into the bathroom to remove my makeup before I showered. As I was getting undressed, Leland appeared in the doorway.

"Have fun being a thot tonight?" he asked slurring.

"Don't start this shit right now Leland. You're drunk, and I just don't have the energy or time to argue with you."

"What you gettin in the shower for? Fucked some other nigga tonight or something?"

"I'm not even going to respond to that!" I told him rolling my eyes turning to get in the shower but yelled when I felt him pull me back by my ponytail.

"LET GO OF ME!"

"YOU FUCKIN' ANOTHER NIGGA? HUH, BITCH?" He yelled, and I fell from trying to get out of his grasp but I couldn't. The more I tried to get my hair out of his hold the tighter he pulled dragging me.

So here I was butt ass naked being dragged throughout my apartment like a fuckin' rag doll while this man yelled at me. Once he got me to our bedroom he let go of me, and I tried picking myself up off of the floor, but in one swift motion, he was on top of me grabbing both of my forearms pinning me to the ground.

"You're hurting me! Stop!" I whined, but he didn't care. I honestly think he gained satisfaction from this.

"You want to be a hoe, so Ima treat you like one!"

"Leland stooopppppp!"

"SHUT UP BITCH!"

"Lelanddddd let go of me!"

"I SAID SHUT UP!" He screamed before backhanding me. He looked possessed staring down on me with spit flying everywhere as he verbally attacked me.

Prying my legs open; I fought to close them. Why did I do that? The nigga backhanded me again before he forced his dick into my dry walls hurting me. Crying I still tried fighting him off, but it was no use because he was bigger and stronger than my 5'0 and 145lb frame.

"Why are you doing this to me?" I asked him crying, but he didn't respond. He just kept thrusting in and out of me.

I was disgusted. In all of the years we've been together he has never violated me the way he is doing now. Yeah, we've fought and tussled a few times but never has he physically hurt me to this degree. I'm not sure what hurt more, him raping and hitting me or knowing that from this night forward things between him and I will never be the same.

****

"Girl from the club right?" the sexiest chocolate man I have ever seen said walking up to me, and I quickly remembered the stranger I had spoken to the night Lauren, and I went out.

"That would be me," I replied bashfully.

"Car trouble?"

"Yeah, my uh tire blew while I was driving. I've been waiting for AAA for thirty minutes now."

"You got a spare?" He asked taking a look at my 2007 Toyota Camry.

"Yes, in the trunk. I just don't know how to change it."

"I'll change it. Pop the trunk for me."

"You don't have to do that for me. I already called for help."

"Yeah but you're standing on the side of the street where crackheads hangout at shorty. Let me help you so you can be on your way, aight?"

"You sure?" I asked looking around, and he was right. School Street and Union was not only busy but definitely one of the worst parts of the city.

"I offered, right? I got you." He said walking around to my trunk as I popped it open for him. Grabbing it, he set it against my tire before walking off and getting what looked like some tools from his car.

He was dressed in some gray Nike gym shorts, a white tee shirt with some white and black Retro 10 Jordan's. His haircut in a low ceaser with his beard lined up complimenting his dark skin. And his lips? Oh, they were so full and juicy looking. I could just suck them off his face.

Listen to me lusting after a man I don't even know. A man who probably had a girlfriend. She was lucky if he really did have one. To wake up to a man as fine as him? Whoever homegirl is she is definitely winning! But damn his lips, every time he licks them all

I envision is him eating pussy. Ain't no way a man with a set of lips like that ain't doing any damages.

Stop Skylen! I chastised myself silently while he went to work changing my tire. I have a whole boyfriend, yet a complete stranger had to change my tire. Talk about pathetic. And yes, Leland and I are still together. It's been a few days since the attack happened and I was still not speaking to him. The next morning, he didn't remember anything that happened or at least that's what he said. I was over it but still leaving him is still proving to be harder than expected.

"You should be good now." He told me standing up. "When's the last time you bought new tires?"

"I don't know. I can't remember."

"You may want to have them looked at. You know, just to be on the safe side."

"I will. Thank you. You didn't have to do that." I smiled.

"It's no biggie. Just make sure you go and have them looked at. I'd hate for this to happen to you again." He spoke before turning to walk away.

"See you around?" I called out to him, and he gave me a lazy smirk before proceeding on to his car.

Shit, I never got his name.

Leland

"Them bitches from the other night hit me up!" My boy Dex told me with some dumb as grin on his face.

"Word? What they talkin' bout?" I asked smoking a blunt.

"They tryna link again, so you already know what type of shit they're on my nigga."

"Them hoes were wild bruh."

"Nah they were some certified freaks. Type of bitches that don't give a fuck where they're at. They're taking one for the team with no problem."

"They're some typical bust downs. Shit was cool, but I'm cool. You enjoy fam." I spoke thinking about Sky.

I fucked up bad the other night. I don't even know what was wrong with me all I know is Skylen, and I got into it. I woke up the next morning, and she had a bruise under her right eye claiming I did it. She was trippin' because I never laid a finger on her in that way. I was so gone that even if I did do it, I wasn't in my right mind.

Them bitches Dex talkin' bout had us doing all type of shit with them. Never in life have I ever tried that many drugs at once. I'm talkin' Molly, coke laced in with the weed and after that everything is pretty much a blur. I don't remember shit. I just know shit was wild.

Back to Skylen though, I loved her, but I wasn't in love with her anymore. In fact, I fell out of love with her almost two years ago. After I lost my scholarship, I fell into a deep depression. Sky finished college but because I didn't have a job she was forced to get one once she graduated. Her parents paid rent on her place the entire time she went to school but vowed that they would stop once she graduated, and they stayed true to that. With me not working she had to, to make sure we were able to survive.

I appreciated the fuck out of her for that, but

after a while I started to despise her. Day in and day out she acted like she had the dick in the relationship and I wasn't feeling that. At the end of the day, all a nigga really has is his pride but letting her take care of me ripped that shit from me. Outside looking in you would think I was mooching off of her. I've tried looking for a job but wasn't shit out there but bullshit ass jobs.

Not only did I lose my scholarship I now had a record due to some bullshit. I was arrested for aggravated assault. I didn't do any time, but I was on probation for 21 months. So of course, whenever a job ran a background that shit always popped up. I just stopped trying altogether. Doesn't make it right but I did.

The sound of the door opening stole my attention for a second and Skylen walked in with a pissed off expression on her face. Instead of saying anything she rolled her eyes and walked through the living room. That wasn't new. This has been her usual for a grip now, just learned to ignore her.

"Aye, uh, Ima get up out of here. I ain't tryna get cussed out by Sky's crazy ass today." Dex said dapping me up before walking out of our apartment.

"Leland, you need to go!" She said appearing in the doorway.

"I ain't going nowhere. Go head wit' that goofy shit."

"If you ain't tryna go then I'll leave just have fun tryna pay this rent!"

"You ain't going nowhere either. Your ass just fuckin' dramatic." I barked getting up from where I was sitting.

"Yeah, okay. Just watch. You got two weeks nigga. Two fuckin' weeks!"

"Or what?"

"You heard what I said. I can't do this anymore. I can't keep paying this high ass rent by myself and you ain't even trying to do anything to help out."

"You've been doing it this whole time, what's the

difference now?"

"The difference is I'm fucking tired! Every day I come home, and your ass is in the same spot! Every fucking day! You know my fuckin' tire blew on the way home today and guess what? I couldn't fuckin' call you because you're useless! Oh, and let's not forget I'm walking around wearing makeup to cover the fucking nasty ass black eye you left me!" She yelled then turned and walked away. I grabbed her shoulder forcing her to turn around, and she tensed up.

"Don't touch me!"

"Why you actin' like this?" I asked her softening up my tone. Without Sky, I didn't have no place to go. My family wouldn't help me. I burnt so many bridges, and Sky was my last hope.

"Ima do better aight?"

"I'll believe it when I see it. You got two weeks to figure something out, or I'm gone. I can't keep living like this."

"I thought you loved me?"

"You really trying to flip this on me right now?"

"I'm just saying. If you love someone, you aren't supposed to give up on them. You giving up on me bae?"

"Leland."

"You really gon' leave me fucked up like this? You know I don't have nowhere else to go. I don't have anyone else. All I have is you." I said to her trying to make her feel bad, and it was working.

I could tell by her facial expression. Her face softened a bit. It no longer held a scowl. She was looking at me as if she felt bad. I needed her until I was able to get my shit together so if manipulating her was what I had to do then that's what I was going to do. It worked this far.

Sen

"Wassup Queen?" I greeted my mother when I walked up to her kissing her cheek.

As always when it was nice out, she was sitting on her porch just taking in the fresh air with a pitcher of homemade sweet tea sitting on the table beside her. Moms lived in the middle of the hood and had no desire to move. I personally believed she enjoyed watching the drama that took place here. Regardless though muthafuckas never fucked with her. They respected her.

"Hey baby, what brings you by?" she asked smiling up at me.

"Nothing just wanted to stop by an see you. You good?"

"I'm always good boy. Ain't nobody going to come around here fucking with me. Even if they did you know I'm with the shits."

"Aight gangsta," I chuckled.

"You better act like you know. You know ya' momma ain't no punk bitch. I used to tear these streets up with ya aunty Tammy!" She stated giggling.

"How you think you turned out the way you did? That's all me right there!"

"I hear you, lady."

"Mmmhmmm. You being safe out here?"

"Of course."

"You better be. I don't need anything happening to you."

"Ma, I'm good trust me. Besides you know me, if I can prevent some shit I will." I told her taking a seat in the chair next to her.

"You need anything?"

"Nah, I'm good. My stamps come in on the 6th and you done already paid the rent up for the year. I'm good baby."

"That ain't what I asked you."

"Jensen, I don't need anything. I'm fine.

Sometimes I think you forget that I'm the parent and you're the child!"

All I have besides Valencia and Grimey was my momma Jennifer. We ain't have much family. She got pregnant with me when she was fourteen. I'm thirty and moms is forty-four. We damn near grew up together. Grams kicked her out when she had me and she's been on her own since. Leaving her to do what was necessary to take care of me. When I was ten, she had to do a bid for stealing. She used to boost for any and everybody who needed fly shit for a low price. For a while, she was good until she got caught and ending up serving two years.

Probably where I got my hustle mentality from. If there was money to get I was going to get to it by any means. Even if that meant taking from someone else's family to feed my own. In this city, the motto was get it how you can and hustle by any means, and that's what the fuck we did to survive. Of course, I didn't plan on hittin' licks forever which was why I was stackin' my bread until I was satisfied to retire from this shit.

As she fired up a Newport 100, I just sat and watched her. Something was on her mind, and she wasn't saying it. I knew my OG well. When something was bothering her, she smoked.

"Wasssup ma?"

"What you mean?" she asked blowing out smoke.

"You're smoking. I thought you quit."

"I did, but sometimes I need it."

"Exactly my point. You only need it when something's wrong. Talk to me."

"Your evil ass grandmother came over the other day."

"And what happened?" I asked.

"She on that shit again. She don't think I know, but I could tell. She said she needs a place to stay."

"You gon' let her stay here?"

"Hell nawl I ain't gonna let her stay here. What I look like? Boo boo the fool? You out of your damn mind!"

"But ma, that's yo momma. You can't do her like that." I chuckled, and she sucked her teeth and put her cigarette out in the ashtray.

"Your point? She never gave a damn about me when she put us out when you were a small child. I haven't spoken to that mean ass lady since I was fifteen. Fuck her. Let her ass go stay with ya aunty Tammy!" She responded irritated

"Ma-"

"Ma hell! Senny I said what I said and I ain't taking it back. I don't owe her ass a damn thing, you hear me? Not a damn thing!"

"Aight, chill. You ain't have to call a nigga Senny though. I'm not a kid anymore." I told her embarrassed. I hated when she called me Senny, and she knew that.

"Boy hush! I'll call you whatever I want to call you. And you will always be my baby don't you start acting brand new!"

After kicking it with my OG for a bit, I finally parted ways with her so I could go home and change for tonight. Money was calling.

Valencia

"Do you mind if I go use the restroom?" I asked dude I was currently on a date with.

"No, take your time Jasmine. I'll be right here waiting." He responded before picking up his knife and fork to cut into his medium rare steak making me gag.

I can't wait until this night was over. I thought to myself as I gave him a half smile. This date was dragging and as you can see I was ready to go. He bored me. Not to mention he reminded me of my grandfather. Yes, the man was that fucking old.

Grabbing my small handbag, I made my way to the back of the restaurant and walked into the bathroom. I needed to get away from that man. Luckily once tonight was over I would be able to dispose of him. For all, he knew I was Jasmine with blonde hair and glasses. He didn't even have my real number. Still, I was nervous. I'm usually nervous before all of my jobs, but this one was different. He was local.

Pulling out my phone, I saw that I had a text

from the guy Tee who I had met at Center Stage. You remember him. Since we exchanged numbers, we've been texting like crazy. I was only supposed to be talking to him to stain him, but the more we talked, the more I wanted him for myself.

I haven't exactly figured out what I'm going to tell Sen so to buy time I'm on this date with this old ass man who owned a cleaning business. I was ready for this date to be over because he was boring me. He keeps feeling on me whenever he sees an opportunity, and it's creeping me out. I swear if he could fuck me right there at our dinner table I'm sure he would.

Reapplying my lipstick, I blew myself a kiss and gave myself a quick wink before parading back out to our dinner table. I was walking like I owned the place. With every sway of my hips men who were sitting enjoying dinner with their prude ass wives couldn't keep their eyes off me. Once I made it to the table, he stood up and reached for my hand letting me know he was ready to go.

Grabbing it the two of us made our way out of

the 350 Grill. The weather was kind of dreary. It was cool. Kind of damp like. Typical weather for New England. As we both stood outside looking at one another, he discreetly placed his hand under my dress, and I cringed as he looked at me smirking. *Fucking pervert.* I thought as I cleared my throat.

"What would you say if I asked you back to my Condo?" He asked me running his finger along my forearm.

"I don't know. You don't think it's too soon?" I asked.

"No. Do you?"

"I mean, this is only our first date. What happened to taking things slow?"

"I'll pay you." He offered. I was getting money either way, so I can careless about him offering me money. I just wanted to play hard to get it.

"I am not a prostitute!"

"I never said you were, but I know money can be very persuasive."

"It's still prostitution."

"I would love to end our evening with a nightcap, but if you don't want to, I understand. Maybe next time." He replied preparing to turn and walk away.

"I'll come," I spoke to him, and a devilish smile manage to spread across his face.

"I was hoping you would. Let's go."

***

"You're so beautiful and sexy." He complimented handing me a glass of champagne.

"Thank you. You're not so bad yourself."

"You know from the moment I saw you, I thought you were one of the most beautiful girls in the world. I just had to have you."

"You're too kind," I replied taking a seat in one of the chairs he had in his living room.

His condo was simple. It didn't seem like he stayed here often though. Everything was spotless. It wasn't over the top decorated. In fact, it was rather plain with the exception of a few paintings and statues.

"I'm serious. You were just looking delicious. I was surprised when you agreed to have dinner with me." He said taking a seat across from me. He was undressing me with his eyes. I could tell, and it was making me a little uncomfortable.

I was no stranger to attention, but this man was coming off as creepish, and I didn't like it. I would be glad when this shit was over. Hopefully, Sen and I come up tonight because I was ready to take a break from this shit. I was starting to feel pimped out. We had enough money to get by. At this point, I was beginning to think this nigga was getting a rush from this shit.

Granted our first lick was my idea but I had no intentions on making this thing a fucking career. I saw a quick come up and figured why not. The nigga was showing off, so his goofy ass deserved to get robbed. That was a few years ago, and we were still doing it.

Excusing myself, I went into the bathroom to freshen up a bit, and to text Sen., I needed him to hurry up so we can get this shit done and over wit. I wasn't trying to fuck this old ass man. He had to be at least twenty years my senior.

Me: Where are you?

Sen: Outside. You straight?

Me: 7th floor apt 705. Hurry up!

Sen: Bet

Deleting our thread, I turned the water on and let it run for a few before turning it off and walking out. Walking out I went into the living room and didn't see him. Walking to check the door, I made sure it was unlocked before walking back over to where I was sitting.

After a few minutes, he came from the back dressed in some silk pajama pants and no shirt. I must admit for him to be older his body was nice. Still, that didn't change the fact that he was a fucking pervert.

"Join me?"

"Excuse me?"

"Join me, in my bedroom." He invited.

"Coming. I just want to get myself another drink. Do you mind?" I asked him, and he said no.

Going into his small kitchen, I refilled my champagne glass as well as pouring him a glass. Pulling out a small vile I emptied some Klonopin I had managed to crush up into his glass making sure to stir it up a bit. Taking a huge gulp out of mine I prepared myself to make my way into his bedroom where he was waiting for me.

I wanted to throw up when I walked in. This man was sprawled out across his bed naked with a damn rose in his mouth. See this the shit I was talking about. Weird creep shit. He was trying to be sexy, and it was just coming off all wrong.

"You waste no time, huh?" I asked walking up to him and extending him the glass I had for him. He accepted it. *This is good. Now just drink the shit so I can fuckin' go.* I thought to myself with a flirty look on my face.

"You must've known I was feeling a little

parched." He said finally drinking from the champagne flute. Surprisingly he finished the whole glass. He'll be floating in no time.

"Just figured I'd be nice. Wouldn't be fair if I had a glass and you didn't. Besides a lady caters to her man." I flirted.

"Mmmm what else does a woman do?"

"Whatever your heart desires."

"Is that right?" He slurred, and I smiled inside. It was game time.

"You ever had your dick sucked while you were tied up?" I asked him going over to his dresser drawers and looking for his ties. Locating them, I grabbed two before walking over to the bed and straddling him. Taking each wrist one at a time, I tied them to each bedpost.

"You ready for me?" I asked but got nothing.

Looking down at him I saw that he had finally closed his eyes. Maybe I overdid it with the mixing of the champagne and klonopin but oh well. I wasn't trying to suck on a wrinkle old dick and play with old balls. Not tonight. I wasn't up for that shit. I couldn't even fathom being on the date with him never mind anything else.

Getting up off the bed I walked back into the living room grabbed his keys and walked into the guest bedroom where he told me he kept a safe. Once I made it to the room, I opened the closet door, and immediately spotted it. Being sure to take my time I removed it from the shelf and sat it on the bed. Opening it my eyes lit up like a kid on Christmas morning. It was filled completely to the top with nothing but money, and I swear my pussy got wet.

Never in my life had we had a lick this big. I'm not sure how much it is just by looking at it, but they were crisps hundreds wrapped up as if they had come from the bank. So, if they're all hundreds, can you imagine how much money this is? Had to be at least a hundred thou easy.

Locating a duffle bag, I emptied the money from the safe into the bag before placing everything back in its place and made my way back to the living room. I spotted Sen at the door nearly scaring the shit out of me.

"Fuck! You scared me!" I hissed.

"My fault. Where he at?"

"Knocked out. Slipped him something and he was out like a light. It was easier than I thought."

"You check the whole place?" He asked me, and I shook my head no.

"You been up here this whole time and you playing?"

"Nigga, you for real? I got a duffle bag filled with money. We don't need to keep looking! Let's go!" I spoke irritated.

"It's only a matter of time before someone sees us. Here. Take this, please. They have all types of security around here Sen."

"You scared?" He asked, and I looked at him like he had six heads.

Was I scared? Hell yeah, I was shitting bricks. I never drugged anyone, and I wasn't sure how long he'd be out or if he would remember anything. So in case, he did I wanted to be gone before anyone saw us leaving his place.

"Look, I know you always take the lead, but this time just trust me. Okay? Please! Take the bag, and I'll meet you outside where we said we would meet."

"You got five minutes."

"That's all I need," I said, and he crept out of the apartment.

Going into his bedroom, I went through the pockets of his slacks and found his wallet. Flipping through it I saw a few bills and took those and his cards. I wasn't going to use them, but I wanted this to look like a legit robbery just in case. I even went as far as opening drawers and throwing clothes around and messing up his living room a bit before leaving him a note telling him I had fun.

He'd never expect me. When he wakes up, he'd think he paid me for my services and kicked me out immediately after. Walking out of his apartment I left the door open and left out the same way that I came in. My job was done.

Skylen

"Somebody decided to come back to work finally I see," Lauren said with an eye roll when I made it to my cubical that was located next to hers.

"I was sick."

"Sick and didn't call me once to bring you anything?"

"I didn't need anything. I ran out and got what I needed and been home since." I lied placing my purse on my desk.

So technically I wasn't sick I was just giving it enough time for the bruise and swelling to go down on my eye. I was trying to cover it up with makeup but the older it got it seemed like, the worse it got. So I told my boss I had the flu. I didn't need people in my business assuming I was a battered woman. Thankfully I never call out, so my boss was completely cool with my absence.

Since my last conversation with Leland, things have been cool. We weren't fighting anymore. We were getting along for a change. He's been apologizing nonstop since that night he hit me, and I was starting to think he was genuine. I mean out of all the years we've been together not once has he ever did that to me, so I just chucked it up to being a onetime mistake.

Like I said before him, and I have history and although I feel like our relationship is over walking away just seems like it's too hard. If I leave him, I'm throwing away almost a decade worth of memories. I was content I guess most would say. Like I knew what needed to be done, but I've gotten so comfortable with how things were. This dysfunction is my new normal.

"Chilli's for lunch? I need a margarita!" Lauren said snapping me out of my thoughts, and I nodded my head yes agreeing with her.

****

"You sure you're okay?"

"Yes, Laur I'm fine," I responded to her.

As promised we went to Chilli's for lunch. Well, I didn't have much of an appetite, and I never drank while working so I guess you can say that Lauren was having lunch and I simply was just there.

"You're acting weird." She spoke taking a sip from her margarita.

"Spill it!"

"I'm fine. I told you that twice already. I'm good. I should be asking you if you're okay since this is the second drink you've had in twenty minutes."

"You keeping track of how much I drink?"

"Nope. Not at all. Just an innocent observation."

"Mmmhmm."

"So you're going to tell me what's wrong or we're just going to act like everything is good?" I questioned with a smirk.

"Nothing. At least not anything serious. You know I'm dramatic."

"Okay.. but that still isn't telling me anything."

"Sky, you get on my nerves you know that?" She said with a fake pout causing me to giggle.

"Here we go with the dramatics. I don't even want to know anymore."

"Good, because I wasn't going to tell you anyways!"

"You're so childish," I said before we both fell out in a fit of giggles.

"Hurry up so we can go back to work."

"Girl fuck that job! They ain't going to fire us."

"Bitch!"

"What? I'm just saying. We've been there the longest. New bitches come and go every day but guess who still here? Our black asses. They'll be alright if we're ten minutes late." She fussed and I couldn't do anything except shake my head. She was right.

While I sat back giggling at Lauren, I felt someone staring at me and there he was. Again. This was getting weird. This is the second time since meeting him at the club that I saw him. A small smile managed to spread across my face but was quickly replaced when I saw Valencia grabbing his hand as the hostess talked to them.

Was he the guy she said was her boyfriend? If he is how the hell did they manage to come together. No shade or anything but Valencia didn't have the best rep when we were in middle school. She was already poppin pussy by the time we made it to the seventh grade. Again, I'm not trying to throw any shade or whatever, but she was a hoe. I mean you heard her when she said she had her child when she was what? Fourteen? But I'm not one to judge.

Taking my eyes off the two of them I sat and listened to Lauren ramble. I can't even tell you what she's even talking about because no matter how hard I try my mind keeps going back to Mr. sexy chocolate. He was fine. I shouldn't even be looking at another man since I have a boyfriend, but I can't help but be drawn to him. He was perfect. At least to me, he was.

"Heeeeeeey Sky!" Valencia greeted me coming up to our table while we gathered our things to go.

"Hey, Valencia!"

"Sorry I haven't reached out yet, I've been so

busy."

"It's okay," I told her just as Lauren told me she was going to the car.

"You want to go and grab something to eat or drinks sometime?" She asked me smiling while he sat down at the booth that was across from me.

I couldn't stop stealing a look at him. He never smiled. All the times I have seen him he had a serious face as if he was taking something in. Like he was processing something. He looked intimidating, yet I couldn't help but feel something. Attraction maybe? Who knows. It was definitely something.

"Sky?"

"I'm sorry, I'm tired. But sure just text me. We can set something up soon. I gotta get back to work. Just hit me up. It was nice seeing you again." I quickly spoke before rushing away from her and out of the restaurant.

"You okay?" Lauren asked me once I got into the car.

"Yeah, why?"

"You look kinda flustered. You sure you're okay?"

"Yes," I responded to her as she pulled off.

I had one thing on my mind, and it was Mr. Anonymous. As bad as this is about to sounds there's something about him that makes me want him. I shouldn't because from the looks of things he and this chick were together, and I had a boyfriend. What the fuck was life?

Sen

"Sooo I've been thinking." Shorty spoke, and I sat back in my seat and looked at her.

"You listening to me?"

"Speak," I replied coolly.

"Uh, maybe we should slow down a bit on the licks. I know money is always the motivation, but I'm starting to feel burnt out."

"Word?"

"Yes, Sen. I need a break."

"I'm not understanding what you need a break from but aight."

"Seriously? You don't know what I need a break from? Sen, you're practically pimpin' me out!" She said angrily. Still, I remained cool.

V was full of shit. It was her bright idea to start this shit from the beginning. I never held a gun to her head and told her she needed to do this shit. She did it because she wanted to. She got a rush out of this shit.

She loved attention. I gave her all the attention she has ever needed, but I don't believe it was ever enough. So when we hit our licks together them muthafuckas fed her ego, and she ate it the fuck up.

So for her to sit here and tell me that I was pimpin her out was pissin' me off. She was making it sound like I was a dog ass nigga but I ain't that. I'm a good nigga. I do what the fuck needs to be done to make sure we're good. But if this is how shorty was thinking, then I could do these missions by myself. Granted she made shit easy because niggas love a pretty big booty thick bitch no matter what the ethnicity. But don't get it misconstrued I can get shit done without her.

"Say less baby," was all I said, and she looked at me confused.

"Sup? What's on your mind?"

"That's all you're going to say? Say less? What is that supposed to mean?" She asked me with a wrinkle in her forehead.

"We good ma. Don't worry about it. If wanting out is what you want then it's done. Don't worry about it anymore."

"Sen."

"We good Valencia. Trust me." I told her just as the waitress brought our food out.

***

"Yooooo!" Grimey yelled from across the street as he leaned up against his whip.

"Sup fam?" I dapped him up while he stood there grinning.

"Fucks up wit you bro?"

"This paper baby! I'm tryna put you on."

"I told you that hustlin shit ain't for me."

"Nah I got something better. Pays way more. You'll get fifteen thou for accepting the job and fifteen more after." He spoke peaking my interest.

"Nigga doing what? For that kind of money, shit sounds serious."

"I need you to eliminate a muthafucka."

"You need me to do what?" I asked him. I needed to make sure that I heard what the fuck I thought I heard.

"I need you to murk someone. I don't care how you do it, I just need the shit to get done."

"Bro, I ain't no muthafuckin' hit man. Fuck I look like? And if I was, you don't even have that type of money nigga!"

"I wouldn't ask you to do something if I didn't think you couldn't handle it." He stated with a serious look on his face.

Grimey was a jokester for the most part. Goofy lil ugly muthafucka. Bro never spoke or moved like this so for him to come to me with this type of proposition shit had to be serious. I just wasn't understanding why he came to me. I was confused than a bitch.

"Lemme think 'bout it. Aight?"

"Don't think too long. Time is money. You know this."

"You gon tell me why the urgency?"

"Nigga violated baby sis. If I do, some shit niggas gon know I had something to do with it. I can't risk it, bro."

"Say less. I'll let you know somethin'."

"Hurry up. I'm tryna get this shit done asap!" He let me know looking stressed out.

"I got you. I'll hit you!" I told him turning around and jogging into the house.

Grimey been my right hand since we were shorties. Anything he needed I got for him and vice versa. Nigga looked out for me when I did my bid no doubt, but he was asking me to kill a nigga. I ain't a killer. I only kill when necessary. But this shit right here he tryna get me to be a part of, I wasn't too sure about.

Money sounded good though. I ain't starving or no shit like that. I got more than enough money to live comfortably for a good minute, but thirty bands is a lot to pass up on. I'd be a stupid muthafucka to let this shit go, but I wasn't trying to go back to jail.

I risked my life every time I hit a lick but murder? That shit was spooky. Like I've said before I only killed when I needed to. Shit wasn't mandatory in my field because we've always kept our shit smooth. So this shit right here was definitely out of my league, but the saying is you can do anything you put your mind to, right?

Leland

Three Weeks Later

"You're late!" Sky said getting into the car slamming the door.

"My fault. I was doing something."

"Doing what Leland? You don't even be doing shit!"

"I had something to take care of. Chill out. I made it didn't I?" I argued. I wasn't in the mood for this shit. I had enough going on already without her nagging.

"Nigga you a whole thirty minutes late and got the nerve to have an attitude like I did something?"

"You stressin' me out yo! Just shut the fuck up!"

"Who you think you talking to with your ugly ass? Hurry up and bring me home so I can put you out my fucking car!"

"Calm down man. It ain't even that serious, and you know it!"

"It is that serious. I've been at work all fucking day! I let you use my car, and you don't even have the courtesy to pick me up on time, and you brought this bitch back on E. You really trying it Le. Like forreal. You dead ass pushing my damn buttons!" She yelled, and I just turned the music up on her ass and dared her to say something else with my eyes.

To be real with you, I had a lot on my mental. Shorty from that night things got out of hand between Skylen, and I hit me up on some let's chill shit. So, of course, I invited her over to the crib. We did what we did, and I told her she had to go before my girl came home. Long story short she been blowin' me up since I kicked her out. Blowin' up my phone, leaving all types of messages and shit.

She even talking about she pregnant. Ain't no way she knocked up. It's only been a few weeks. I know that hoe ain't pregnant this fast. She tryna straight pull an okie doke on me and I ain't with it. Told her if she is pregnant she better get rid of it because I don't want any kids. I can't afford them shits no way.

Not to mention Skylen would kick me out if she even got wind to any of this shit. I know I said I'm not in love with her anymore, but I need her. At least for right now. I can't afford to lose her yet, but once I get my shit together, I'm dippin' immediately. All we ever do is fight. I haven't even slept next to her in about maybe four, five months. Shit is just different.

I needed to get my shit together fast though because for the past few days I've been feeling like something bad is going to happen. Like there's a storm brewing. I'm not sure what's going to happen, but shit was getting dark. I could feel it.

"You need anything before we head home?" I glanced at her briefly as I drove.

"Nope, just take me home so I can get from around your selfish ass." She said with an attitude not bothering to look at me.

"I told you I was sorry for runnin' late. I got

caught up with some shit!"

"Whatever Leland. Just bring me home and stop talking to me. Seriously. I'm fucking tired. My head hurts, and I just want to go to bed."

"Bet," I told her and continued on the route home as my phone buzzed letting me know I had a notification.

I was happy inside because as soon as she dozed off, I was leaving again. I had shit to do.

***

"Yeah suck that dick," I groaned looking at her head going up and down in my lap.

"You like this baby?" She asked glancing up at me and winked before going back to giving me some super sloppy head.

Lil bitch was a baddie. She thick ass fuck too. Only thing is she had a man. She only fucked with me whenever shit was convenient for her. I only fucked with her because she be lookin' out for ya boy. Especially since Sky wouldn't.

Grabbing a fistful of her hair, I forced her head deeper into my lap so that my dick could touch the back of her throat. I wanted her to make my shit disappear. That and the fact that I loved to hear her gag. For some reason, that shit was so sexy to me. By the time she finished toppin' me off her makeup was smeared all over her face.

"Fuccccckkkkkkk girl!" I groaned lowly closing my eyes.

I was about to cum. I could feel the nut building up at the top of my dick. She could too because she started sucking on the head harder until she finally sucked my cum completely out and swallowed it. Once she was finished, she smiled before getting up and giving me a quick peck.

"I gotta get ready to go home. You can stay here for the night if you need to. The room is already paid for. You need anything before I go?" She asked me as she fixed herself.

"Just a couple of dollars. I'll lace you when I get some bread."

"Don't worry about it."

"Nah, you know I got you when I get right. That's my word." I promised.

"I told you not to worry about it." She said again giving me a few benji's preparing to make her departure.

"You a real one. You know that?"

"I don't know how to be anything else. I'll talk to you later baby!"

"Let me know when you make it home." I told her, and she winked her eye at me before leaving out of the room.

She was wild. Going home with dick all on her breath. This is why I treated women the way I did. They degraded themselves by doing the shit they did and dealing with bullshit. But Valencia, baby girl was a straight bust down, and her man was a clown if he thought he had a trophy.

Valencia

Let's make love in the summertime, On the sands, beach sands, make plans

to be in each other's arms, yeah. Let it breathe. I wanna drown in the depth

of you, yeah yeah.

I drove all the way home with Jay-Z and Beyonce's Summer playing on repeat. This song put me in such a zone that every time I listened to it I envisioned life with the man I was supposed to be with. And that man wasn't Sen. Sen is cool, but I want more. I want and need stability. I want someone whose eyes twinkle when they look at me.

He and I have been together for a few years now, and our lives have become so routine. I was becoming bored with it. We did the same shit day in and day out. After our last lick with that old nigga, I was ready for some different shit. I was trying to get him to see that we didn't need the money. We were good. Even if we weren't straight for the rest of our lives, we were good for a few years.

Not to mention that nigga Tee I had met that day him, and I are still texting and talking to each other whenever we got the chance. I was starting to like him. He wasn't your average hood nigga. He had goals and ambitions. He was already preparing to make his exit and I liked that about him. He's a man with a plan.

Granted when we first met, he was supposed to be a lick. Nothing more nothing less but I can't fuck up a potential meal ticket in case shit comes to an end with Sen and I. You can never be too prepared. I had plans on meeting up with him tonight, but some shit came up, and he had to bail last minute, so I hit up my other little boo thang Leland.

Leland is nothing more than a fuck, to say the least. He was so needy, and I didn't do needy men, but the nigga dick was fucking amazing. His problem was that he's broke as fuck. I'm talking broke with a capital B. So, whenever him and I hooked up I threw a couple of dollars his way. I guess you can say I was paying for dick because that's all he had to offer. He don't know it yet, but I have plans on breaking it off with him soon. He has way too much baggage for little ol' me.

The whole time we were kickin' it tonight the nigga bitched and complained about his girlfriend that I did not give a fuck about. I didn't even know her name and didn't care to. That's just how much he meant to me. He also mentioned something about some girl claiming to be pregnant by him and that was it for me. He was too messy. How can a whole nigga be that muthafuckin' messy?

Nevermind. I'll tell you how. Because it's fucking Springfield and all these bum ass niggas do is fuck bitches and stir the fucking pot. I could not stand that shit! No matter what part of the field you were from, these niggas was messy and bitched more than the bitches do.

Speaking about this city, I wanted out. I was tired of this shit hole. Every time I turn the damn news on someone has either gotten killed, or a kid is missing and later being found in the fuckin' Chicopee River. Shit like that put a damper on my spirit. Even now with me talking to you about it, I managed to get depressed. I needed a pick me upper. I needed to do a line.

Finally making it to Sen and I house that we were renting. I opened my purse and pulled out my stash and did a few lines before putting a little bit on my gums. Sitting there I allowed the high to consume me for a few minutes before I got out the car and made my way inside. When I got in the house, Sen was sitting on the sofa with everything off looking like he was in deep thought. I didn't have time for this shit tonight. I am not in the mood for a philosophy lecture. I was floating, and I had no plans on coming down just yet.

Throwing my purse on the loveseat that was close to our front door, I walked past him and into or dining room before finally making it to the kitchen where I poured me a shot of Patron.

"Where you been?" He asked from behind me scaring me.

"You didn't have to scare me like that!" I said

turning around and looking at him.

He was biting down on his back teeth. His jaw was flexing. He was mad. I understood that. But I wasn't going to stand here and have this conversation with him. I didn't want to and not to mention to fucked up too.

"Where the fuck you been Valencia?"

"I was out."

"Out where? Stop fuckin' playin' with me."

"I just said I was out! Get off my fuckin' back Jensen! The fuck!" I yelled before trying to walk away, but he grabbed me by my elbow stopping me.

"Let go of me!" I demanded, but his grip got tighter before taking his free hand and turning my head to look at him.

"Bitch is you high?" He asked noticing the glossy look in my eyes, but I didn't say anything. Instead, I dropped my head.

I wasn't ashamed that I sniffed. I mean I wasn't

proud either, but it is what it is. I pop Molly from time to time, and when I don't have Coke, I pop percs. Anything that can help me escape my reality I did it. I've been doing it since after our first lick. I was just able to hide it.

I've always been a drinker. Ever since I was a kid. My biological mom was and still is a crack head. She never gave a fuck about me. If she did, she wouldn't have introduced me to alcohol when I was eleven. She was the cause of my addiction. I ended up pregnant by a man she sold me to just to get high. My aunty Michelle at that point had, had enough. So I moved in with her, and she's been raising my daughter as if she was hers.

I didn't want Harmony. She reminded me of everything that I went through as a child. Not to mention she has down syndrome. I couldn't care for her the way mama could. Yes, I called Michelle mama because she has been a better mother to me than my own dead-beat ass mother. Still, for the life of me, I couldn't get my shit together nor do I even have the desire to.

Sen shoving me snapped me out of my thoughts. He was angry which was understandable. He had every right to be. His woman was a junky. In his eyes, that's what I was to him. A typical junky. Even if I told him I have everything under control, he would still look at me with the disappointment that he's looking at me now with.

"YOU OUT HERE ON THIS SHIT?!" He barked with spit flying out of his mouth.

"ANSWER ME!" I was so high I couldn't even respond. Between the coke and the tequila, I was on some next level shit.

Once he realized I wasn't going to respond. He just walked away from me and out of our house. He'll get over it.

Sen

I had to leave Valencia's high ass before I layed hands on her. I knew about her occasional pill poppin shit, but she was on some other shit tonight. She was on some coke. Stupid ass didn't even realize she still had residue under her nose.

One thing I don't do is junkies. I had no respect for them. They would do any and everything to get high, and for that, I always looked at them as weak. I didn't feel sorry for them either because getting high was a choice. Valencia had a fucking choice about whether or not she was going to get high. And it would be a matter of time before her addiction got the best of her. Look at her dumb ass can't even talk. Probably still in the same place stuck where I left her.

I was disappointed. I ain't even gon lie. When I turned her around so that she could face me, I felt like my heart was breaking. Shit ain't sweet with us, but they aren't bad either, feel me? We go through our share of shit but was it that bad to turn to drugs? I didn't understand.

If I was one of those fucked up niggas I probably would have fucked her ass up, but I would never lay a finger on a woman. I'll cuss their ma'fuckin' asses out though. But physically hurting one? Nah that ain't even in my character. I'm surprised I shoved her ass. I had to get the fuck away from her.

When I hurried and got the fuck out of the house, I didn't know where I was going, but somehow someway I was now sitting outside my momma's crib feeling played. Not only was she high as fuck but I could smell another nigga on her. She was out here living foul. She could very well have been looking for new targets, but after our conversation the other day, I highly doubt that. So not only is my bitch a junky, she cheating too. Type of shit is that?

Getting out the car I walked up to my mom's crib, using my key I let myself in and crashed on the sofa. My mind was all over the place, and I was sure sleep wouldn't find me.

***

"What you doin' here boy?" my OG asked when I woke up.

Stretching. I yawned before responding.

"Got into it with ol' girl."

"What happened this time?"

"Nothing,"

"Nigga I woke up and you were sleeping on my couch sounding like a damn grizzly bear. You got ya own shit to lay up in, the hell you doing here?"

"Ma."

"Ma hell. What happened? Lie again, and Ima kick ya ass out. You cheating or something?" She asked, and I lightly laughed.

"Nah, you know I ain't built like that. I'll leave before I cheat."

"That's what all you niggas say."

"Did you just categorize me?"

"You a man, ain't you?"

"Yeah but-"

"But nothing. I know what y'all are capable of doing!"

"I ain't cheatin' ma. You got my word. She came home mad late high as fuck and before I snapped I had to get from around her stupid ass." I confessed sitting back replaying last night's events in my head.

"High? What you mean high? Off weed? She smoking that kush or whatever the hell y'all callin' it these days." She asked lighting up a Newport.

"Nah, coke. She was geeked. Eyes bucked and glossy as fuck. She was so gone she was stuck."

"Oh, so she gettin' high? Wow."

"Right. Fucked me up. Ma you know how I feel about people that use drugs."

"I understand that but baby, some people are fighting demons we have no idea about."

"I don't want to hear none of that shit."

"Watch ya mouth boy."

"My fault mom, I'm just saying. Ain't no excuse for her to be out there doing that shit; I mean things she has no business doing."

"Jensen. Baby, sometimes people do things, and we have to accept that. May not be things we're proud of, but we need to let them be. That girl is troubled. I could tell the first time I met her. A dark cloud follows her everywhere she goes. Son, she is fighting demons you have no idea about."

"So, I'm supposed to just sit back and watch her self-destruct?" I asked confused.

"No. You support her. If you love and cherish the relationship, the two of you have you're supposed to help and support her. If this isn't a relationship you think is worth fighting for then you let it go. My mother chose drugs over me, so I left her where she was. I couldn't continue to fight for someone who didn't have it in their heart to fight for me." She spoke before standing up.

"I raised you to be a strong black King. You

know what you need to do." She finished saying before patting me on my shoulder and leaving me alone with my thoughts.

Things between Cia and I have been strained for a while now and to be honest, I wasn't sure where the two of us was headed.

Skylen

I was so tired last night that I came home and passed out. I woke up around three in the morning and Leland was nowhere to be found. His light skinned ass even took my car without my permission. I was sick of the dumb shit. Here it is now eleven, and he had yet to return with my car. He wasn't even picking up my phone calls.

He stood in my face and told me he was going to do better and like a fool I believed him. He did good for about a week before his old habits returned. I couldn't do this shit anymore. I just couldn't. I rather be alone than to feel alone in a relationship.

Pretending and putting up a front was starting to become draining. Mentally and physically and it was starting to show. He didn't deserve me. He didn't deserve me giving him chance after chance to get it together. He didn't even deserve the love I have for him at this point either. So instead of continuing to call him, I called Lauren, so she could help me change these locks.

Leland had some place to stay because if he didn't staying out all night would be an issue. So, all I wanted from him was to bring me my car and get the stepping. I was officially done. If I have to choose between loving myself and loving him, I will always choose me first. Seems like he always chose himself first anyways so staying in this dumb ass relationship was complete and utter bullshit.

Going outside to check the mail, the weather was beautiful for a fall day. It was a nice seventy degrees. Kids were outside playing already. Some of them didn't have on any jackets which irritated me, but I wasn't too surprised because I saw shit like this daily in the hood. Especially where I lived. The Bergen Circle projects were right up the street where majority of the kids lived.

Grabbing the mail, I walked back up to my porch before the neighbor waved at me. She was a middle-aged black woman. She was alone most of the time. I never saw any kids or anyone come visit her, but she always smiled. Whenever she saw Leland and I together, she would look at me in pity, and my stomach always turned. Everyone except me knew that he was no good for me.

Before I made it back inside, she called my name, and I looked at her confused for a bit before she waved me over. Against my better judgment I went over to her fence.

"Hey, Ms. Jennifer! How are you?" I asked smiling at her.

"Hey, pretty girl! I saw that boyfriend of yours sneaking out the house last night. Bastard took yo damn car too. I was going to call the cops!" She said firing up a cigarette making me laugh.

"What time was this?"

"About midnight I believe. I see his narrow ass still haven't made it back yet!"

"He must've snuck out when I was asleep. I've been working overtime and yesterday I came home and passed out." I told her embarrassed, and she gave me that look. That same look of pity that I didn't like.

"You called me over here, is everything okay?" I asked changing the subject.

"Oh, I'm sorry. I start ranting and get off topic. Forgive me." She giggled before looking into her house.

"Jensen! Come here, boy. Let me introduce you to someone." She yelled and shortly after he came to the door looking yummy as ever and I started feeling that tingly feeling inside again.

"Sup ma?" He asked in a raspy voice.

"I want you to meet my neighbor Skylen." She said to him pointing in my direction, and when he saw me, he looked like he seen a ghost.

"Skylen this is Jensen, baby this is Skylen."

"N-n-n-n-nice to meet you." I stuttered embarrassed as hell. I never stuttered a day in my life, and now my dumb ass decides to in front of this beautiful chocolate man.

"Nice to meet you too." He smirked.

"Ma, you think you slick, huh?"

"I don't know what you're talking about."

"Yeah aight. You ain't low."

"Well uh, I'm going to head home. I'm waiting on a friend to take me to the store." I told her getting ready to walk away.

"I'm sure my son wouldn't mind taking you, right?" She asked him, and he shrugged his shoulders before responding.

"Nah I wouldn't mind. I gotta get myself together, but if you still need a ride when I'm done, I don't mind bringing you wherever you need to go." He offered and before I could respond Leland pulled up in my car pissing me off.

Instead of responding I walked off and snatched my car door open when I made it to my Camry. Reaching inside I snatched my keys out of the ignition and put them in between my titties. He wasn't bout to take these bitches again!

"The fuck is wrong with you?" He asked with some bass in his voice pissing me off even more.

"You been out all night and have the nerve to ask what the hell is wrong with me? Are you fucking kidding me? Leland go. Just fuckin' go! You clearly don't want to be here!" I yelled.

I don't even do the public fighting thing. My business was my business, but I just didn't give a damn today. I was sick and tired of being sick and tired. Ain't like the neighbors didn't hear our arguments any damn ways so fuck it.

"You showing out in front of these fuckin' neighbors! Let's go in the house Sky!"

"Oh noooo. You won't be stepping foot in MY house today or any other day! You gots to go! I don't care where you go, but you need to leave!"

"I ain't going nowhere. This my house too!"

"Bitch you don't pay shit in this bitch! Bye Leland! Go back to whatever bitch you were with! You smell just like somebody's rotten ass pussy!" I shouted and walked away, and he pulled me back my shirt.

"AYE, LET HER GO!" Mr. chocolate aka Sen

yelled jogging down his Ms. Jennifer's porch steps.

"MIND YOUR BUSINESS. THIS AIN'T GOT SHIT TO DO WITH YOU!" Leland yelled back still not letting go of my shirt.

"Let go of my shirt Le! How can you be mad but you're the one staying out all night! Let go of meee!"

"I told you to let her go, right?"

"Nigga, fuck y-" he started to say but didn't get the chance to let the you come out of his mouth because this scary ass nigga had stalled on him just that quick with no warning.

Leland wasn't much of a fighter. He was raised in the suburbs. He ain't no shit about being in the hood. I don't even think he even been in a fight. While he was trying to regain his composure. Sen grabbed him and put him in the choke hold before whispering something in Leland's ear. Not even gonna front, I was scared for him. The pain was written all over his face. After a few more seconds of them tussling Sen finally let him go but not before duffin' him in the face knocking him out.

By this time, I was amused, and embarrassed all at the same time. There was people all outside watching everything that had taken place, and I instantly regretted starting a scene outside. I just knew I was going to be the talk of the hood for a few days. Instead of helping Leland up, I locked up my house and got into my car, so I could go to Lowes to grab some locks. I meant what I said. I wasn't dealing with Leland's shit any longer. I rather be lonely than miserable.

Valencia

I was crashing. I was finally coming down from my high, and I was hating it. After Sen and I's disagreement, I did a few more lines and popped a pill just to numb myself. I knew why he left, but I didn't have it in me to even go after him. What good would that have done? He was already angry.

Picking myself up off the couch I got up and went into the kitchen. My throat was dry. I hated when I was coming off a high. I usually binged for a couple of days, but I had a date tonight. I was finally seeing Tee, and I couldn't wait.

Glancing at the clock on our microwave the time read 1:34. We were meeting up around six, so I needed to get myself together quick. Since everything that transpired between my man and I you would think I'd stay my ass home but nope, not me. Tee hit me up right after Sen left and we agreed to see one another today.

Walking throughout our place, I went into our bedroom and sat on the bed and looked straight into our closet. How did we get here? When Sen and I started out we were inseparable. Wherever you saw him, you saw me too and vice versa. Somewhere down the line we just drifted apart so now the two of us we're just coexisting in this relationship.

Still, neither one of us left, and the higher I got the less the drift affected me. That along with other things had my mind occupied. Michelle was sick. She called me a few weeks ago telling me she was diagnosed with Stage three lung cancer and it was time for me to step up and be a mom to Harmony. Being a mother wasn't in my plans at least not to a child with such disabilities.

At first, I figured okay maybe I can do this but the more reality sets in, the more I begin to panic. I'm not mother material. I'm not sure if I'll ever be. I enjoy being able to go whenever the hell I feel like it. Or only having to look after myself. Harmony needed too much attention. Attention that I couldn't give her.

Does that make me a horrible person? Selfish even? Maybe but I didn't have time to care for anyone else other than myself. So, by all means, think what you want about me, but it will not change my mind about what I said. Period.

At the end of the day, I am a grown ass woman living my life the best way that I could possible before I couldn't anymore. I didn't have time for things or people who would potentially get in the way of that. Sen included.

Speaking of him he hadn't even tried to get in contact with me. I'm not surprised, but I am surprised. Does that make any sense to you? We've argued plenty of times before, but he'd still text me to make sure I was okay. He didn't do that this time. I don't even think he's as angry as he is disappointed. He looked hurt. I do remember seeing that look on his face.

He would never understand the things I deal with daily mentally, and never will he know. Truthfully, I wouldn't even bother explaining anything to him. For what? So he could act like Captain Save A

Hoe?

The sound of the front door opening let me know that he was here. Crazy how I was just thinking about him, and he comes home, right? That's low key spooky. When he came into the room, he just looked at me before going to our closet without saying a word and that kind of hurt.

"Sen.." I called his name and with his back facing me, he responded dryly.

"What?"

"You leaving again?" I asked when I saw him grab a duffle bag.

"Valencia, I can't be around you right now ma. You came up in this bitch higher than a muthafuckin' kite. Not to mention breath smelling like some nasty niggas dick. You out here doing me bogus." He spoke putting things in the bag.

I opened and closed my mouth about four times trying to say something, but nothing would come out. Even when he glared at me, I couldn't say anything. I was mute. I swore I managed to put myself together before I left Leland at the hotel. I thought I popped a mint as well. Fuck!

Contrary to what you may believe I never wanted to hurt Sen. He was a good nigga. He has his flaws and shit, but for the most part, he was good to me. I may not want to be with him anymore but hurting him was never my intentions.

"You need to get your shit together with your goofy ass. Go to rehab or some shit!" He spat before walking out and leaving me alone.

Damn.

Sen

It took everything in me not to spazz out on Valencia. I dead ass wanted to choke the fuck outta her, but I wasn't that type of nigga. She thought a nigga was going to talk to her, but I ain't have shit to say to her dirty ass. This the woman that I've been rocking with for years and with all this new shit coming out I felt like I didn't even know her.

Fuck all that though. I've been thinking about that proposition Grimey had hit me with. I could use the thirty g's to add to my stash I already had. If I'm counting off the top of my head, I'd say I had about seven hundred thou saved up. Not bad for a nigga from Springfield. Valencia didn't know that because I kept my shit at my mom's crib.

Speaking on my mom, she thought she was slick. She was tryna set me up with shorty I met at the strip club a few weeks back. Shit was crazy. The first time I have ever seen her was there, and it seems like ever since that night I kept seeing her pretty ass. At least now I had a name to put to a pretty face.

Baby girl seemed cool. I don't know her story but after that shit with her and ol' boy earlier I felt bad for her. She ain't deserve for a nigga to treat her like that. And with the way he grabbed her, I know the corny ma'fucka had broke his foot off in her ass a time or two. If I wasn't out there he would've done that shit again with no remorse.

I wasn't gon' interfere until I saw him grab her. I don't ever involve myself in other people's shit, but something about her made me want to save her. Crazy, right? I got a woman, and I'm out here playing captain save a hoe to someone else's. The comedy. It was just something about her that kept me wanting to know her despite her relationship with dude. I want her. I shouldn't, but I do.

Stopping at the gas station off Saint James, I got out the whip and walked into the store. Grabbin' a Minute Maid Cranberry juice and some Lemon heads I waited in line when I noticed this base head walking around touching my car. Placing my money on the counter, I hurried up out the store and made my way to my shit.

"Aye, you lookin' for somethin'?" I asked, and they picked their head up and a knot formed in my throat. It was my grandmother. I never had a relationship with her, but moms made sure I knew who she was. Judging by the look on her face she needed a hit. She looked sick.

"You have some change young man?" She asked oblivious to who I was, but instead of answering her back I got in my whip and pulled off. I wasn't contributing to her fucking habit.

Soon as I made it to my mom's crib, my mans called. I knew what he wanted. He was tryna see if I decided to do him that solid and I was. I just needed all my money up front. I was going to do it on my terms, my way. I was just hoping like a ma'fucka that it wasn't someone we knew. Springfield is small as fuck. Everyone knows everybody. And everyone who is somebody pretty much rain in the same circle. I ain't fuck wit' too many cats cause I wasn't with that extra shit, but I was well known.

"Yooo," I answered picking up the call as I sat looking at Skylen's crib.

"Sup wit' it muthafucka?" He asked hype.

"Ain't shit, just pulled up at mom's crib. Sup?"

"I'm bouta slide through."

"You good bro?"

"I'm smooth, I need to rap wit' you though. I'm bouta slide through."

"Aight, bet," I said hanging up just as Skylen pulled up in front of me.

She sat in the car for a while on the phone. Seemed like she was arguing with someone. I knew this because she had a whole bunch of hand movements going on. After a while, she finally got out and opened her back door grabbing a few bags, and immediately I jumped out and made my way to her taking the bags from her hands.

"You didn't have to do that." She shyly responded placing a piece of hair behind her ear.

"It's cool. I wanted to."

"I never thanked you for earlier. I appreciate that. You didn't have to jump in."

"Nah he was bein' wild disrespectful. Plus my mom's wouldn't even be cool wit me standin' by watchin' some shit go down like that."

"Momma's boy?" She questioned with a giggle and her dimple threatened to peak through.

"I wouldn't say all that, but I definitely respect my OG," I responded as we both started walking to her front door when we heard someone call her name.

"Sorry, I tried to get here as soon as possible." The girl apologized before turning her attention to me.

"Who's this?"

"Aren't you nosey," Skylen said to her friend unlocking the door grabbing the bags and placing them in the doorway.

"But since you must know this is Sen, Sen this is my friend Lauren." She introduced us while Lauren looked me up and down before going into the house.

"Sorry about that."

"It's cool. What you bouta do?" I asked her fishing.

"Changing my locks and probably having a drink. You?"

"Shit. Maybe I can come check you before you call it a night later?"

"Sure, we sitting on the porch though."

"It's your world gorgeous; I'm cool with that."

"Okay, guess I'll see you later." She said smiling and going into the house.

"If it ain't the flyest nigga in Nebraska!" I heard Grimey joke, and I turned around and jogged down her stairs and walked up to him.

"I see you got jokes and shit today," I told him leaning up against his whip.

"So wassup, what you want to talk about?"

"You marinate on that shit I asked you to do?"

"Yeah man..."

"And?"

"I'll do it, but I need all my money up front."

"Type of negotiating shit is you on?"

"Nigga you askin' me to murk a ma'fucka. You know I don't kill unless I have to."

"I hear you. I'll get you your bread and shit just make sure you get on this shit like yesterday, ju heard?" He stated seriously.

"You already. So, what's the name?"

"Leland."

"Type of name is Leland?" I asked trying to figure out where I heard that name from.

"Shit muthafucka, I don't know. From what I heard the nigga corny ass fuck, but he has a problem with disrespect, and you already know I don't take kind to that. He hurt my sis, so the nigga needs to be dealt with."

"Heard you."

"Aight man," he said as his phone rang. Looking down at it he let out a frustrated sigh.

"I gotta go, man, I got some shit to handle. Ima get you ya bread and shit. Have sis lace me with a photo so you can know who you lookin' for. I'll get with you."

"Say less," I told him dapping him up.

After this shit, I was laying low. Probably figure out my next move. I had enough money to be straight for a while. Maybe even relocate to another city or something but then again who knows. This type of shit keeps my adrenaline going.

Skylen

"You going to tell me what happened and why we changing locks?" Lauren asked me as I started unscrewing the original locks on my door.

"Leland stayed out all night. He waited til I was asleep and took my car."

"You know where he was?"

"Girl, no. But the nigga came here like everything was okay around noon time with not one care in the fucking world. I'm tired of him disrespecting me." I vented feeling stupid.

I had these conversations so much with Lauren they were beginning to sound like deja vu. I was getting tired of hearing myself talk about the same thing over and over again. And I'm sure she was getting tired of hearing it. I can't believe I wasted damn near ten years on a relationship that should have ended a long time ago.

"Sky if you're going to go back to him changing these locks won't solve or fix anything. It'll be a complete waste of time."

"I'm not going back."

"Is that right?" She asked giggling as if she didn't believe me and I didn't blame her. This isn't the first time I talked about leaving him and ended up staying. However, this time felt different.

"I just can't do it anymore friend. He'll act right for about a week and then it's back to the same shit. That shit is toxic as hell, and he straight got me out here looking goofy as fuck. Besides the nigga put his fucking hands on me and I don't play that shit!" I revealed without realizing until it had already come out. *Damn Skylen, you talk too fucking much.* I cursed myself silently inside.

"Wait, run that back. He did what?!?"

"Nothing."

"Bitch stop playin' with me. You got this Trey Songz wannabe nigga laying hands on you, and you ain't say nothing? Seriously Sky? Since when did we start doing that?" She asked disappointed, and I remained silent.

I never had any intentions on telling anyone that. That was something I planned on taking to the grave because I was embarrassed. Embarrassed because I always said I would never be that girl, but here I was. I allowed a man to not only harm me physically but emotionally and mentally as well.

"You don't hear me talking to you?" She asked, and I just sat down on the floor near the door.

"Sky, talk to me."

"It happened a few weeks ago. Up until that day he has never put his hands on me. I mean he's grabbed me up a few times but to hit me? Nah that never happened until then." I confessed with my head down.

"Look," she said sighing and taking a seat next to me on the floor.

"He was wrong as hell for hitting you. You didn't deserve that no matter what you did. Even him grabbing you up and shit is a no-no. A man who genuinely loves you for you will never hurt you. I ain't saying he's going to always be perfect, but he will never harm you if he loves you no matter the situation. You hear me?"

"Lauren I don't even know how we got here. I don't even know when it got this bad."

"Girl shit been bad for a while now you were just blinded by the amount of time the two of you had together. I'm not here to judge so I let you do you, but if he's putting hands on you, I hope that you're done for good. Besides Mr. Sen looks like he's smitten with you."

"Lauren."

"I'm just saying. Even a blind man can see the chemistry and attraction the two of you have." She said bumping her shoulder with mine.

"He has a whole girlfriend. He ain't thinking about me."

"Who? That bitch you call yourself reuniting with? Trust me, he ain't thinking about that girl."

"How you know?" I questioned confused.

"Because bitch the nigga wouldn't be sniffin' around your ass. Y'all keep running into each other. That ain't a coincidence. That's fate."

"The hell you know about fate?"

"Nothing but I know y'all not just running into each other just for the hell of it. The universe is talking. You better pay attention and listen. Besides the best way to get over some old dick is to get under some new dick. Just make sure you throw that ass back and thank God while you do it." She said making me laugh.

"You're nuts, you know that, right?" I asked laughing.

"I'm just being honest. Now let's hurry up and get these locks changed before Leland walks his ugly ass in here."

"He ain't coming in here today. Sen beat his ass earlier in front of every one girl. That nigga is ashamed!"

"So you tellin' me sexual chocolate beat your

boyfriend's ass, and you ain't give him no pussy? And this shit ain't fate? Yeah okay. You better wake up and smell that fucking Tequila we about to body."

"What is wrong with you girl?" I giggled while she stood up before helping me up.

"Bitch I need to be asking you that. Your future boo beat up your current boo and you in here playing. The nerveee chile the fuckin' nerve." she joked.

***

Knock! Knock!

It was a little after ten, and someone was knocking at my door. I had a feeling already about who it was, and it made me nervous. I was trying to get Lauren to stay the night, but she said something about going to see one of her boos, so I gave up with trying to convince her to stay. Instead, I've been sitting here nursing a drink while I watch Love and Hip Hop Hollywood.

Getting up from where I was sitting, I threw on my hoody and slipped on my Fenty slides before stepping out into the cool fall air. He had already made himself comfortable on the top step, so I just sat next to him. Neither one of us spoke for a few minutes. We just sat in silence.

"You good?" He asked finally breaking our silence.

"I'm cool. You?" I asked just above a whisper.

"I'm straight. That nigga come back and fuck with you again?"

"Nope, I think he was humiliated."

"I didn't even do shit to him. Shit could've been worse. I'm just glad you're alright."

"I am. You made sure of that."

"I mean, I don't like shit like that. I'm sure after he cooled down and shit you would've spoke to him, but he just went about shit all wrong, and shit pissed me off. I'm sorry if I stepped on your toes and shit."

"You're fine. Trust me," I replied and it went back to being silent again which was fine.

For some reason, I found comfort just being next to him. I felt protected. The nervousness I had felt before I came outside had long gone away. He wanted to say something. I could feel it. He was fidgeting with his hands. That was always universal for anxiousness.

Placing my hand on top of his I stopped his movements, and for a brief moment, the two of us made eye contact. Sen wasn't what you would call the finest, but he wasn't all that bad either. His aura that he carried is what drew me to him, and his physical came second. He wasn't Leland, in fact, he was the complete opposite, and that made me drawn to him even more.

Looking at him I could tell that his story went far beyond his eyes and it made me curious. It made me want to get to know him despite him being involved with Valencia. Was I wrong for being curious about this being sitting to the right of me? Maybe but I didn't care about that.

"What's your deal?" I asked him removing my hand from his.

"What you mean?" He asked back with his

eyebrows knitted making him appear intimidating.

"What's your story? You always helping people you don't know? You have saved me on more than one occasion."

"Nah. I don't even like people to be real with you. That day I changed your tire I couldn't just drive past you. I remembered you from the strip joint, so I stopped. Today though, shit wasn't going down while I was a few feet away. Whatever y'all got going on is between y'all two, but when it gets to niggas grabbing women and shit, I gotta intervene."

"I hear you."

"How long you and ol' boy been together?"

"Eight years."

"And how old are you?"

" Twenty-six," I responded looking up at the moon.

"So he's all you know. I dig it. But peep, any nigga that's willing to treat you the way he did in front of muthafuckas don't give a fuck about you. He handled you wrong earlier."

"Sound like Lauren. She says this to me all the time. I guess I've gotten used to it."

"You should never get used to a ma'fucka mistreating you. These niggas gon' treat you the way you let them. If you ain't got no respect for yourself, they ain't gon respect you either. You gotta change shit up. I know I don't know you or no shit like that, but I'm a man, so I'm putting you on game." He spoke pulling out his ringing phone.

Standing up he stretched before turning and looking at me. He didn't say anything he just stared like he was peering through my soul causing me to get uncomfortable. So I broke our eye contact and just stared at my boots.

"Ima get going, go inside. Too late for you to be sitting out here by yourself." He said jogging down the steps.

"Good night Skylen. I'll be in touch."

"You don't even have my number."

"I don't need it. You ain't hard to find." He chuckled nodding his head in the direction of my house.

"Go in the house shorty."

"Good night Sen." I smiled getting up from the spot I was sitting in and going into the house. Today was one eventful day, huh?

Leland

One Week Later

"Fuck you keep calling me for?" I yelled into the phone to Niecey. Chick who claimed to be pregnant by me.

"What's your issue with me?" She asked pissing me off.

I had enough shit going on. Last week Skylen put me out. On top of that, she changed the locks, so I couldn't get my things from our apartment. So now I was crashing at my boy Dex house. He was cool, but I didn't feel right living with a bunch of other niggas. It just wasn't my thing. So Niecey calling me just pissed me off even more.

"You get rid of that problem or you still on some bullshit?"

"I told you I'm not getting a fucking abortion! And even if I was who's paying for it? Your bum ass can't!"

"So if you know I can't pay for a fucking abortion then why the fuck would you keep a child when we're both broke, does that make any sense to you dickhead? Besides you got health insurance, they'll do that shit for free."

"Don't worry about it! I don't know why I gave you some pussy anyways. You only lasted three fucking minutes anyway. Me and my baby don't need you nigga. I hope when my brother catches you he fucks you up!" She yelled into the phone before hanging up.

I was completely unfazed by her tantrum. Niecey was dumb as fuck. She was the type of bitch who would cheat on a test and still fail every single question. I often wondered if she was slow or some shit because the shit she did was questionable. For example, keeping a child that neither one of us could afford. She had Mass Health, so I don't know why she was hell bent on not getting rid of it.

Besides I didn't like her like that. Things weren't even supposed to get that fat between the two of us.

We did what we did, and that was it. I could have sworn I used a condom but then again, I was so geeked up I don't remember much from that night nor did I want to.

Finishing getting myself together I was preparing to go meet Valencia. She been looking out for me though since all this shit happened. She even got me a rental to get around in. I was hoping she'd get me a room for a couple of days to crash, but I didn't want to seem too needy.

No bullshit I liked Valencia stuck up ass. She wasn't shit, but I couldn't help but be attracted to her. In my opinion, her and I was one of the same. She would probably disagree, but I stand by my thoughts. If you asked me her and I belonged together. I don't know the type of nigga she's in a relationship with, but he had to be some corny ass nigga if she was fucking around on him.

Grabbing the keys, I walked out of the house without saying anything to anyone. I was on my way to the Residence Inn by Marriott in West Springfield. She was waiting on me. As long as I dropped this dick off in her, a nigga could get whatever it is he wanted.

***

"Valencia?" I called out to her when I walked into the suite she had gotten. I stopped at the front desk like she told me to and got the keycard but now I'm confused because it doesn't look like anyone has even been here.

Placing everything on the little table near the door I walked around from the sitting area to the bedroom and the bathroom still coming up empty-handed. Pulling out my phone I dialed her number, and she picked up on the third ring.

"Where you at?" I questioned.

"I had to stop somewhere for a second. I'm coming now, baby."

"Stop where?"

"Nosey are we?" She flirted sounding intoxicated.

"I'm just saying, you told me to come here and you ain't here."

"Relax Leland, I'm literally down the street. I'll be there in a second."

"Aight," I said and hung up.

Walking to the sitting area part of the room I sat down on one of the single chairs and turned the TV on. I wasn't watching it, I was too deep in my thoughts. I needed to figure out what I was gon do. Since Skylen wasn't fucking with me, I needed to make moves. This couch surfing shit wasn't me.

I could have been back home with my parents, but that would be the last result. If I could avoid that move, I will at all cost. Something had to give. It just had to. Ain't no way I was out here living bad like this.

Not gonna hold you I'm stressed as fuck right now. Times like this is when I hate that I was kicked out of school. I didn't know what to do. I didn't have any hustle in me but this dick. I knew my dick game was proper and the right bitch would be able to finesse. Look at the situation with Skylen. I've been able to fake shit for a while now because I had just that much power over her. My dick was the reason for that.

Speaking of her let me give her ass a call. It's been a couple of days since I last tried calling her. Hopefully, she hadn't blocked my number yet. If she did, I knew things between us was a wrap. If I call and her phone rings, I still have a shot with her. Right? Dialing her number it rang four times then went to voicemail instead of leaving a message, I just hung up.

"Why you sitting here looking all sad?" Valencia asked me walking into the room.

"I'm cooling."

"No, you're looking like you lost yo best friend or your girlfriend."

"You got jokes or somethin'?"

"Just an observation. So you never told me why you needed my help. I'm here now so talk to me."

"Nah. It ain't serious."

"I can't help you if you don't tell me why. I

already got you a rental without asking questions."

"I told you it isn't that serious."

"Cut the shit Leland, what happened? Your girlfriend left you or something? You ran into some trouble? What is it?" She asked taking a seat across from me and crossing her legs, but I didn't say anything.

"Fuck it. I had booked the room for a week for you, but since you don't want to tell me what the fuck is going on, I can go back and get my fucking money back!"

"Chill. You buggin'!"

"Nah, I'm not, but you are if you asking me for help expecting me to do something without asking questions. It's my money paying for this shit!"

"Shorty kicked me out! You happy?" I said angrily. She was pissing me off.

I hated having to ask bitches for shit because they thought they ran every fucking thing. She asking questions like the shit really mattered when she was already planning on helpin' a nigga out. I was starting to think that these hoes just enjoyed complaining about shit.

"Oh, that's it? I figured when you started calling and texting me nonstop. Speaking of which what happened to us being discreet?"

"What you mean?"

"You know what I mean. You know you can't be calling and texting me all freely. I have a man. You know this." She spoke, and I waved her off.

I was going to get what I could from Valencia and move on. Fuck her and Skylen's selfish ass.

Skylen

If you don't know how to treat a woman close your eyes,
ain't no point

in looking over here with that weak shit. Get out of here with
the weak

shit. You won't get nowhere with that. I had your type
before, no I don't

want that back. Don't want that back. You talk fiction, I talk
facts.

I was packing Leland things up and donating his shit to The Salvation Army. He wasn't getting anything that I bought him back, and that pretty much was everything he had here. I was serious about moving on with my life. I had already wasted years, and I had no plans on wasting any more.

Crazy thing is I suspected that he was cheating, but I never had solid proof, well not until he stole my car and didn't return til the next day. That right there was a dead giveaway, and god himself couldn't tell me otherwise. I won't front and act like I'm not hurt because I am. The man I planned my life out with was acting all out of his character doing bogus shit like I meant nothing to him. Like our relationship meant nothing to him.

So instead of continuing to sulk around, I decided today is the day to get his shit out of here. For the first few days, it was hard not to respond to messages and phone calls because every apology sounded sincere. However, in the back of my mind I knew better. I knew not to fall for the same lies again.

It was time for me to be single and just relax a little bit. I didn't need the headache and hassles of trying to maintain a relationship while trying to figure myself out. Not to mention Sen and I have been talking here and there whenever we ran into each other. He was cool, but he also had a girlfriend, so I wasn't even trying to get too deep into him.

Packing up the last box, I put it out on the front porch in front of my door along with the others before standing up and putting my hands on my hip. It was getting cooler, so there weren't as many kids out. The ice cream truck had just pulled onto my street like it was ninety degrees and not the sixty-two that it was.

"Moving?" Ms. Jennifer asked me being nosey. Smiling I responded.

"No, just getting rid of some stuff."

"Some stuff?"

"Yes. I did some cleaning. Getting rid of everything that doesn't belong here anymore."

"Want me to have Jensen come get it?"

"No, they're going to The Salvation Army." I answered with a sigh.

"I can have him take them Skylen, it's okay."

"No. I don't want to be a bother."

"Girl hush! I'm going to have him put them in your car as soon as he gets here."

"You don't-"

"Didn't I tell you to hush Ms. Thang?" She asked before smiling until her phone rang.

"I don't know what the hell this damn woman wants. I told her naggin' ass I'd call her when I got settled in now here she come callin'!" She fussed going into the house, and I did the same.

As soon as I got inside Lauren was calling me. Since everything between Leland and I had gone up in flames, she has been super supportive. She's been calling, and even at work the other day I walked in to a sticky note telling me how amazing I was. That meant a lot to me because it was the little things that I appreciated.

"Hey boo!" I answered with a smile as if she could see me.

"Hey, hoe. What you doing?"

"Nothing just finished cleaning and packing you know who stuff up."

"You really went through with it?" She questioned.

"Yuppp! I told you I was."

"I know, but damn I wasn't expecting you to

move so quick."

"The way I see it the quicker I got his things out of here, the sooner I can start coping," I responded.

"You're right. Well, what do you plan on doing with his stuff if you don't mind a bitch asking."

"Donating it. I'm pretty sure someone else can wear the shit."

"Okay, Ms. Petty. I'm scared of you!"

"Shut up. You so silly. What you doing?"

"Nothing. Out at the Outlets buying some shit. It's dead out here though."

"That's because you ain't bring me with you."

"You wouldn't have came anyways so don't even go there."

"You don't know that bitch."

"Sky. You don't like leaving the house. Your ass wasn't going nowhere. Besides, I only came to Lee Mass. I didn't go to Wrentham." She spoke, and I felt a little better.

"Well bring me back some candles from Bath and Body Works since you out there. I know they got a sale going on." I told her just as there was a knock on my door.

"Hold on girl somebody knocking at my door."

"Bitch don't be opening doors without asking who it is! Michael Myers might be on the other side and I ain't there to save you!"

"Would you shut up?" I laughed opening the door and there he was standing at 5'7 in some jeans and a basic ass white and tan Champ hoodie and Timbs on his feet.

"Can you unlock your car?" Sen asked, and I felt a heartbeat in my clit. I swear for gawd every time this man was around me I got horny. I just wanted to sit my pussy lips on his juicy sexy lips and fuck his face. Excuse my language, but he did this to me every single time.

"Uh, sure hold on."

"Bitch who that?" She whispered as if they could

hear her making me laugh again. Unlocking the car with my alarm, I watched as he picked up one box and placed it inside of my car.

"Sky! You don't hear me? Who is that?"

"Sen.."

"Who?"

"Bitch Sen.."

"Who the fuck is.. Ohhhh sexual chocolate. What he doing knocking on your door?"

"Damn you all in my fuckin business ain't you?"

"Don't be rude because you in front of company." She sassed as I continued to watch him.

"Bye Lauren. Call me when you go to Bath and Body so I can tell you what candles to get!" I told her and hung up just as he was finishing up.

"What you doing with the boxes?" He asked standing in front of me again.

"Dropping them off to The Salvation Army."

"True, dude been round here again?"

"I don't think so. I'm at work most of the time so he could possibly come by while I'm there, but he can't get in. I changed the locks."

"You changed them yourself?" He questioned with his eyebrow raised.

"Yes, why?"

"You don't strike me as a woman who can use tools."

"Are you saying I'm a kept woman?"

"Nah I ain't saying that. I'm just saying judging by your looks I don't see you fucking around with hammers and shit."

"That's why you shouldn't judge a book by its cover." I flirted, and his phone rang.

"I gotta answer this. I'll catch up with you later beautiful."

"Okay," I said watching him tell whoever it was on the other line that he understood before hopping in his car and speeding off.

I have to stay away from his chocolate ass because whew chile the things I would do to that man!

Sen

As much as I wanted to stay and talk to Skylen, I had to jet. The sun had finally gone down and today was the day that I took care of that problem for Grimey. Nigga came through and gave me all my money up front, so I was gon' keep my word. My word was bond, and that nigga was my right hand.

Speaking into the Bluetooth hookup in my car I requested to call him to make sure I had the right place. Nigga had me going to a hotel, and that shit was risky as hell. Cameras was everywhere in that bitch, and the last thing I needed was to get jammed up in some shit.

"Talk to me." He answered.

"Nigga I ain't one of ya bitches."

"My fault I didn't even see that you were calling me. Wassup? We got a problem?"

"You sent me the address to a hotel ma'fucka!"

"Word?"

"Yeah, nigga. You want me to murk the nigga in a building full of cameras?" I asked sitting outside the place.

"Nah, what's the name of it?"

"Residence Inn in West Springfield."

"Stay put. I got a lil shorty that work at the front desk. Let me see if she at work." He said and hung up.

I wanted to get this shit done and over with so that I could go holla at Valencia. I hadn't spoken much to her except for a few messages here and there. I thought about everything mom dukes had said, and she was right. I either needed to help shorty or leave her alone, and I wasn't a nigga who was quick to give up, so I was willing to try as long as she got the help she needed.

Valencia thought that I didn't know about her past, but I did. At least I knew what I could dig up. I found out about her daughter not too long ago after a strange number kept calling back to back. Instead of answering she kept drinking like she ain't hear her phone. I got tired of the shit ringing, so I picked up.

Yeah, that was some hoe shit but fuck it. I did what needed to be done. I spoke to her aunt and shit. She told me everything and then some. At first, I was upset about it until I processed it all. I figured I'd give her some time to come around, but she never did that. Still, I was willing to work things through with her even if I was kinda diggin Skylen.

Skylen was a different story. She was so green to a lot of things, and I liked that. She lived in the hood, but she was far from a hood booger. She definitely had some hood in her, but from what I gathered from her she was a lover with a whole lot of love to give. With her, things flowed differently. She was cool to kick it with.

The sound of my phone chiming caused me to look at it, and it was a message from this nigga Grimey.

Grimey: You got ten minutes nigga.

Me: Bet

After responding to him, I memorized the room number before making my way inside of the lobby where shorty behind the desk slid me a key card without saying a word. *This ma'fucka Grimey got bitches doing all type of shit for him.* I thought to myself while walking straight to the elevator. I waited until it opened and pressed the number five for the fifth floor. Once I was on the floor, I followed the room numbers until I got to where I needed to be, putting a pair of gloves on before entering.

Sliding the key card into the door, I saw that there was a sitting area as soon as you entered. He was here because clothes were scattered everywhere. Not only were there clothes everywhere moans could be heard from where I was. The moans sounded familiar, but I shook that off and attached my silencer on and sliding a face mask over my face.

I had ten minutes probably seven now to get in and out before the cameras were turned back on. So this shit was going to be quick and easy. Nigga was so into fuckin' his bitch he didn't even know his life was in danger.

"Shitttt this pussy so fuckin' wet!" This lame ass

nigga groaned sounding like a bitch. Nigga was doing more moaning then the bitch was.

Annoyed and running out of time I let off two shots to the back of his head making him collapse right on top of whatever bitch he was fucking. Screams filled the room while she struggled to move his heavy body from on top of her. As much as though screams sounded familiar, I couldn't even dwell on that. I had to hurry and get the fuck up outta here.

Exiting the room as quickly and undetected I had entered I took the stairwell downstairs and made my way to the lobby. When I made it there, it was still empty, and ol girl was still stationed there, so I slid her the key card and walked outside and got into my whip.

Me: Done

Grimey: Good looks.

Pulling away from the hotel I couldn't stop thinking about who that voice belonged to. The more I thought about it, the more it made me want to figure out who it was. Then suddenly it came to me.

"Valencia?" I questioned myself out loud but as quick as that thought had entered my mind. Couldn't have been her, right?

Valencia

I couldn't move. I was still covered in his blood. I still had a little bit of brain matter on me. Paramedics and police officers had been trying to get me to talk for the past twenty minutes, but I couldn't. I was numb.

We were having sex. Enjoying one another in the moment. You know doing the nasty. I was so close to climaxing and next thing you know he's dead. Someone had killed him. Right in front of me. With no remorse. They were probably after me and got him instead.

I've done a lot of fucked up things to people my whole life, and it's only a matter of time before Karma has its way with me. Leland didn't bother anyone. Or at least that's what he told me. He was a square honestly so who would want to hurt him? That hit was meant for me.

How did I know it was a hit? Because they didn't even take anything. My purse was right at the door. They came in did what they needed to do and got the fuck outta dodge. Not to mention I hit licks with my nigga for a living so this shit wasn't random.

The police officer that arrived first to the scene took a seat next to me before taking a deep breath.

"You ready to talk yet?" He asked, and I rolled my eyes.

"All I need is a brief statement on what happened. Can you give me that? Or you can come down to the police station. Choice is yours." Again I said nothing I simply got up and grabbed my keys and purse and left. I wasn't no fucking snitch. Even if I was there wasn't shit to tell them other, then the nigga had a black mask on.

***

"Hey, this is my third time trying to reach you. I really need you right now. Can you just come home when you get this?" I spoke into the phone leaving Sen a voicemail.

After leaving the hotel I came home and scrubbed my body down, but it did no justice because I could still smell his blood. I could still feel his brain matter being on me, and every time I closed my eyes all I saw was him falling on me with his eyes wide open.

I've seen Sen kill plenty of people in front of me, so I wasn't a stranger to it. However, this just seemed different. Maybe if he wasn't killed the way that he was, I would feel differently, but then again, I don't even think that would have made a difference.

My body was tired. I needed sleep, but I couldn't sleep. I refused to fall asleep without my man being here to console me. I couldn't tell him what was going on, but I could just have him hold me. That's all I wanted anyway. I wanted him to hold me. I needed and wanted to feel safe.

Not being able to sit still I went and found my stash of coke. I needed to get high. That's the only way to calm myself. I didn't want to deal with my reality. I didn't want to deal with too much of anything I just wanted to wait until Sen came home. I know things have been sketchy between the both of us, but whenever I needed him, he always came. Always.

No matter what he was doing or who he was with he came running. No questions asked. I remember when we lost our baby. I didn't want it, but he did, and I entertained the idea of keeping it only to turn around and lose it shortly after. I was crushed. I remember it like it was yesterday.

***

"What's wrong? You good?" He asked me on the phone.

"Sen.. there's blood. I don't.. I don't know why but I'm seeing blood." I said in between deep breaths. I was cramping so bad. I could barely stand up, and blood was just seeping through my pants.

"On my way! Where you at?"

"Bathroom. I can't move. It hurtsss. It hurts so badddd Sen!"

"Calm down. Can you do that for me? Can you just relax a little bit? Hmm?"

"Fuccckkkkkkk!"

"Shit! Valencia, I'm on my way! I'm on my way, you

hear me?" He yelled into the phone, but I couldn't answer. I was too busy cradling my stomach.

This was pain I had never felt before. I went from cool to hot in a matter of seconds. I felt like someone was pulling on my uterus and wouldn't stop. This shit was the worst. I've read about people losing thier child in the beginning stages of their pregnancy, but I didn't know this is what it felt like. The more the cramping hurt, the louder I yelled while I waited on bae to get home.

It seemed like forever before Sen had finally made it home to me. Immediately he got on his knees all while trying to console me, but I didn't want to be touched. Instead, I told him to call my doctor and tell her what was going on.

The look on his face told me that he wanted to take the pain away, but he didn't know how. His face also told me that he knew that we were losing our child at that moment and that crushed my heart. This wasn't supposed to happen.

***

"He's coming. He has to. He always does." I spoke to myself while the cocaine did its job traveling throughout my bloodstream.

Sen's coming home. He loves me.

Skylen

"Soooo are you going to tell me why chocolate was here earlier?" Lauren asked, and involuntarily I blushed.

"He wasn't here technically he just put the boxes in my car."

"But why did he put the boxes in your car? You asked him to?"

"Bitch no. I was putting them on the porch so I could carry them myself and Ms. Jenn saw me and told me she'd have him to put them in the car when he came by, so he did."

"Mmmhmm sureeee."

"I'm serious. I never asked him to do that. I don't even talk to him like that."

"Don't seem like it to me. He sure has been around a lot lately."

"And your point?" I asked sipping my Patron.

"My point is that the two of you are getting pretty close for two people who are in relationships."

"Hold up. Let me stop you right there. I am single as of last week. He, however, is dating my friend."

"Girl Bye. She is hardly your friend. You haven't heard from that girl since y'all left middle school." She replied popping her tongue.

"It's still wrong though. I'm cool with the friendship we've been trying to establish."

"Sky. Let me ask you a question."

"What? And it better not be stupid either."

"You wouldn't fuck him if the opportunity presented itself?"

"NO!" I damn near shouted.

"Are you crazy?"

"It's just a question girl, chill. I think you're lying though. I bet money that you would pop that pussy if he asked you to."

"I am not a hoe. Don't do me!"

"Bitch you don't have to be a hoe to let a nigga splash all in that thang. Shit if it was me, I'd be poppin coochie all over his chocolate ass. Lucky I dip more in the lady pond then I do the man pond." She winked sipping her drink.

I told Lauren that I would never fuck Sen, but truth be told I found myself fantasizing about him earlier after he left. Remember I said every time I'm around him he does something to me, and I meant that. My pussy got a heartbeat every time he was in my vicinity.

So, hell yeah I thought about fucking him. I wasn't going to admit that to Lauren though. That was my business, and she didn't need to know that. But best believe if it were to happen she would be the first and only person to know. Okuuurt!

"You all up in my business what's going on with you heffa?" I asked changing the subject, you know taking the heat off me.

"Nothing. You know I don't be doing shit. My life consist of work, shopping, chilling with you and fucking."

"So raunchy! So nasty!"

"I'm classy. Never raunchy hoe." she yawned looking at the time. It was a quarter past ten, and we both had to work in the morning at nine.

"Ima get going before my ass calls out tomorrow. You tryna hit up Fat Cats this Saturday night though?"

"Fat Cats? The hell we going there for?"

"To have fun. And it's free. Why not?"

"You know I don't even go downtown that often."

"Girl, you need to get out the house more. We can go there then hit the casino right after. Might mess around and find our sugar daddies while you playing."

"I am not about to play with you. Seriously. Bye Lauren!" I said, and we both stood up at the same time.

"Your ass going out this weekend. I don't care what you say! Live a little Sky! You're single. Start doing single women shit!"

"You act like I'm not currently dealing with a breakup!"

"In my eyes y'all been broken up for years but you ain't hear that from me. Ima get going though." She said walking to the door opening it with me following her and Sen was getting ready to knock.

"See you at work tomorrow girl. Maybe. It might be a good night." She said giggling and getting into her car.

"My bad, I didn't know you had company."

"It's cool. You okay?"

"Yeah, I'm straight. You mind if I come in?" He asked, and I moved to the side allowing him in. Babyyyy let me tell you I was shaking like a whore in church.

I have never had any other man in my apartment other than Leland. We moved into this place with each other. His scent was still lingering around especially after going through all of his things. It was as if he had just left.

"So wassup? Everything good? Is it your mom?" I asked after closing the door and turning to face him.

"Nah, moms cool. You cool?"

"So why are you looking like you have something on your mind?"

Instead of responding he walked right up to me, grabbed the bottom of my face and crushed his lips against mine before I could even register what was happening. Gosh his lips felt so good against mine. They were so soft and juicy. I could still taste the Carmex he had on his lips.

"W-w-w-w-what just happened?" I asked tripping over my words.

"I just want to fuck the shit out of you. Can I do that?" He asked in a husky tone, but my voice was stuck in my throat. Of course, I wanted him too long stroke me until I was cumming and speaking in tongues, but he had a girlfriend. I couldn't do that to Valencia even if we weren't the best of friends. It was too close for comfort.

Then again part of me was curious and wanted to know if he would fuck me the way I dreamed that he would. I wanted to know if he would live up to the expectations. However, at the same time I was scared. And did I mention just morally wrong for obvious reasons. I couldn't do it yet when he grabbed my hand and led me to the couch I couldn't protest. Well maybe I could have, and I didn't want to.

"Sen.," I whispered as we looked at one another in the eyes.

"We can't do this," I spoke still not trying to move out of his embrace or taking my eyes off his.

"If you believe that, I'll walk out that door without saying another word. Is that what you want shorty?" He asked, but I didn't answer. He was calling my bluff.

After a few more seconds of looking at each

other and battling with myself, I just reached for his zipper, but he pushed me down on the couch beneath me. Before dropping to his knees and spreading my legs. This was the one time I was happy that I decided to wear an oversized t-shirt around the house with no panties under. He had VIP access to my love garden.

Feeling him bite on my inner thigh sent me through a brief frenzy. His bites weren't hard, but they weren't gentle either. They were just the right amount of pain mixed with a little bit of pleasure. As he bit and sucked his way up my thighs his head occasionally grazed my pussy lips turning me on. Releasing a slight moan, I secretly wanted him to place his succulent lips on the set of lips he was getting ready to lock eyes with.

Once he reached my opening, he looked up at me winking before he dipped his head back in between my legs as he began tongue kissing my pearl. And he licked me like he hadn't eaten in days and I was his favorite meal that he couldn't get enough of. As my breathing became heavier, I closed my eyes and enjoyed the pleasure he was giving me with his mouth.

"Mmmmm," I moaned causing him to pull my clit in between his lips sucking it hard, and I didn't want him to stop. If he kept this up, I would be cumming in no time.

"Yessss, ohhh yes!"

"You taste so fuckin' good." He said in between licks as he lapped up my juices like he was a dog drinking water. I just pushed his face deeper into my wetness.

"Oh, my gaaawwddd! Please don't stop!" I begged, and I meant it.

I didn't want him to stop. It's been so long since I had a man cater to my body and needs the way he was doing. I've been with Leland for so long and thought I'd never experience anyone other than him, so this right here was one for the books. Out of all the sessions he and I had they have never been this intense.

As Sen continued with his tongue beating on my pussy, I think I thanked God a thousand times in my head for this very moment. He was eating and sucking me so good that my juices had formed a puddle underneath me.

Sticking one of his fingers into my pussy he never once stopped sucking on my now swollen clit. He was driving me crazy, and he knew it. I was squirming trying to back away from him feeling myself getting ready to cum, but he locked his arms around my legs keeping me stuck.

"I'm about to cum! I'm about to cum! I'm about to cummmmmmmm!" I panted as my body started to shake.

Sen

Chuckling I removed my face from between Skylen's legs watching her clit pulsate. Little pussy got wetter than a bitch too. I still could feel her juices on the tip of my nose as I continued to watch her standing up to my feet and stepping out of my sweats and briefs.

I probably was wildin' right now, but I can't front, I've been wanting to bend her over since the other day. She was coming in from work and had on some tight ass dress pants, and that thang was poking. Ever since that day I have envisioned myself sliding in between her walls from behind.

Once she came down from her high after that orgasm, she locked eyes with my dick, and I could've sworn I saw her swallow hard as hell when she saw what I was working with. Yeaaaa, a nigga was working with a monster. I wasn't the biggest, but I wasn't tiny either. I was a solid nine inches and maybe about two inches in width. That's probably why she looked like she had seen a ghost.

Still, I stood there and grabbed my shit and stroked him slowly. She couldn't keep her eyes off me no matter how bad she wanted to peel her eyes away from my dick, she couldn't. I had her ass stuck. Before she could protest, I slid a condom on and joined her on the couch. I was uncomfortable for a little until she moved a bit and within seconds I was slowly inching my way into her opening.

"Ahhh," she groaned, and I stopped witnessing the discomfort on her face.

"Want me to stop?" I asked her. I was real life hopin' she would say no because I just knew her pussy was gon' be some fire.

"No.. Just be gentle please." She said softly, and instead of responding I rubbed the tip of my dick against her opening before sliding myself in slowly. And maybe because she was already anticipating it or the fact that she tried relaxing herself a bit I was able to get myself halfway in. If I wasn't used to pussy I probably would have came prematurely.

Her walls was grippin' my dick something serious. I knew her pussy was going to be tight, but she would have had you thinking she was a virgin with the way her pussy was hugging my dick. Moving in and out of her I watched as her face went from looking like she was in pain to ecstasy.

"Sen."

"That shit sounds so sexy coming from your pretty little mouth. Say that shit again." I spoke to her never stopping.

"Oh Sennnn," she moaned wrapping her legs around my waist as I continued to move in and out of her.

"This shit feels so fuckin' goooood!"

"Can I put it all the way in?"

"Mmmhmm."

"You sure?" I asked, and she bit down on her lip as she nodded her head yes and without warning, I slid my dick all the way into her wetness hitting her cervix; giving her all nine inches.

"Fuuucccckkkkkkkk!" She cried gripping onto my shoulders.

I've had plenty of pussy in my day. Knocked down some of the prettiest bitches but this girl right here? She was something different. My dick fit into her perfectly along with the wetness of her shit she had my head spent. I wasn't usually a quick pumpin ass nigga, but I could feel my nut at the tip of my dick.

I hadn't even been inside her no more than two minutes, and already I was about to bust, but I couldn't do that yet. I stopped stroking resting inside of her before kissing her. I wasn't a kissing ass nigga, but I had to do something other than look at her sexy ass underneath me.

"Fuck me Sen, please!" She begged so I pulled out and told her to arch her back, and she did without asking questions.

Once her arch was just right, I spread her ass cheeks and just admired how pretty her pussy looked bent over. She was sloppy wet, and without warning, I slid into her and started giving her long strokes. The way her ass jiggled whenever she fucked me back fucked my head up a bit. Shit had a mind of its own.

"Ohhhh shitttt! Right thereeee. Oh, right thereeee!"

"You like this shit?" I asked slapping her ass.

"Oh God yesssss! Yesssss! Just don't stopppppppp!" She moaned as I hit her spot repeatedly.

I wanted to cum, but I needed her to cum first. I wasn't bout to let her hoe me. A nigga's toes was cramping up because I knew that this nut was about to be the biggest nut I've ever had.

"Sennnnnnnnnnnn, oh Sennnnn!"

"Sen what? Huh? Sen what?" I asked in a throaty voice never stopping.

Gripping the back of her neck, my pace slowed down a bit, and I closed my eyes. Every time I watched her throw her ass back, I felt like I was goin' to cum. Mind you her shit wasn't as fat as V's but bent over her shit was beautiful.

"I'm about to cummmmmmmmmmmm!"

"Cum then, fuck is you waiting for? Cum all over this dick!" I coached her and within seconds she was splashing all over my shit. I wasn't too far behind because almost immediately I spilled all of my seeds into the condom. I rested inside of her for a bit before pulling out of her and sitting on the couch next to her.

Neither one of us spoke. Both trying to catch our breath. The mood in the atmosphere had changed just that quick. Glancing over at her she had a blank expression on her face. I couldn't read it, and that made me uncomfortable. I didn't want shorty to think I solely came over to fuck her when it wasn't even like that. I wasn't on that type of time with her.

"I'll get you a rag." She spoke and got up coming back a few minutes later.

Removing the condom off my dick she took it from me, and I wiped my shit off before getting dressed. Grabbing my keys, I turned when I heard footsteps. She was standing in the kitchen doorway wrapped up in a towel.

"You're leaving?"

"Yeah, I gotta get on out of here and you gotta work, right?" I replied to her, and she didn't say anything. Instead, she walked to her front door and held it open for me.

Making sure I had everything; I walked to her door where she was standing and kissed her forehead. I'm sure me leaving wasn't what she expected but I wasn't going to lay up, and pillow talk with her. I needed to head home. Valencia kept blowing me up earlier, so I was going to check her out. Last time she did this she miscarried our child.

I may not be fucking with her as tough right now because her dumbass don't know how to act but I still have an obligation to her. We were still together, and I haven't been home since that incident that happened recently, so it was only right that I went.

"You aight?"

"I'm fine. Good night Sen." Skylen replied damn near pushing me out the door and closing it.

Instead of trying to figure out what was wrong with her I walked to get into my whip, and my mother was outside smoking a cigarette. She shook her head at me.

"I know you didn't do what I think you did!" She said, and I just smirked and got into my car.

"I did , and it was well fucking worth it," I spoke out loud to myself before pulling off.

Valencia

It was a little after midnight when I heard the front door open. It was Sen. I had called him hours ago, but all my calls went unanswered. I should be upset, but I'm not. He was here now, and truthfully that's all that mattered to me.

Twenty minutes later he came strolling into our bedroom with a towel wrapped around his waist. He was different. I hadn't seen him in about a week or so, but I knew that something was different. It wasn't anything physical that was different. The energy that eluded from him was off, and I didn't like it.

Everything inside of me was telling me he was seeing someone else. I could feel it. I sensed it. When he came into our house, his first stop was the shower. Maybe he had just slept with her? But why come home? Or maybe he had saw her earlier during the day, and her scent was still lingering on him? Whatever it was I can guarantee you that he was seeing someone else. My woman's intuition was going off.

"Sup?" He asked with his back facing me while he slipped on some pajama pants to sleep in.

"I've been calling you all day."

"I've been busy, you straight?"

"Yes," I lied.

I wasn't straight. In fact, I was mourning my lover. I was mourning my relationship. Not to mention Tee wasn't answering for me. I was fucked up. I felt like I was living someone else's nightmare. My world was falling down all around me. I felt like I was suffocating. I couldn't tell him that. Not without admitting to my infidelities.

"You was blowing me up because you're okay? Valencia does that make any sense to you?" He asked taking a seat on the edge of the bed. Still, his back was to me. I wanted him to look me in my eyes.

"Why won't you look at me?" I asked him, and he released a frustrated breath.

"Mannn fuck was you blowing me up for? I

thought some shit was wrong but you sitting here trying to play twenty-one questions and shit."

"Excuse the hell out of me if wanting to see my man is a fucking crime!" I yelled jumping out of bed.

If he wasn't going to turn around and look at me, I was going to make him look at me. Stomping over to him I stood in front of him with my arms folded. I looked crazy as hell. I had my natural hair up in a puffy ponytail, pajama shorts and an oversized t-shirt.

"I'm not about to argue with you!"

"Jensen where the fuck have you been? You fuckin' someone else? You've been gone for a week and some change!"

"Ayo, you serious right now? I can go if you want because I didn't come here for all of this shit." He responded cooly finally looking at me.

For a while, the room was filled with complete silence, and then my phone notification went off. Instead of him saying anything he just grabbed a pillow and walked out of our bedroom. It's like he knew it was a nigga texting me, and when I picked my phone up, it was Tee.

***

I didn't sleep an ounce last night. I couldn't every time I tried to I saw Leland being killed in front of me. I guess this will be my normal for now, huh? I did talk to Tee via text message last night, and I wasn't feeling him anymore. He was trying to get me to come out because he wanted some pussy again.

I fucked him the night we went on our date and after that I hadn't heard much from him. He took me back to his place over in West Hartford, we had dinner did a few lines and next thing you know a bitch was bussing it open. The nigga was cheap as fuck though. I asked him for three hundred dollars to get my bundles installed, and the nigga laughed in my face. I didn't need his money it was a test to see if he would give it to me. He failed. Still, I was like he's cool so let me play my cards right.

But after how he switched up on me after getting some I've been plotting on robbing him since.

Yesterday was the final straw. I called and texted him all day telling him I needed a friend, and he ignored me. When he finally did reach out to me, all he wanted was some pussy, and I wasn't about to let some corny ass nigga play me like I was fucking whack.

So here I was sitting at the kitchen table trying to figure out how I was going to do this shit. I couldn't do it alone. I needed Sen, but I just told him not too long ago that I didn't want to do this shit anymore and at the time I didn't. I really wanted out, but I needed to teach Tee a lesson. According to him, nobody knew where he lived so he would obviously know it was me, but I didn't care. I was slitting his throat as soon as he put two and two together.

I could probably do this job alone, but Sen was the muscle that I needed. In case anything went wrong he was there. But with the way things been going on between us, I wouldn't be surprised if the nigga told me no. This would be my last job for real this time. I just kept feeling like something was going to go wrong eventually and before it happened, I wanted out. Just not before I got Tee's ass.

"Good morning," I greeted Sen when he walked into the kitchen and going into the fridge to grab a Gatorade. Instead of greeting me back he just nodded his head in my direction.

"I was thinking. Remember the guy from the strip club?"

"What about him?"

"Let's do it."

"I thought you were done with this shit."

"I am. After this one."

"What you up to V?" He asked never taking his eyes off of mine, and I hated when he did that staring shit. It has always made me uncomfortable.

"Nothing," I said slowly.

"Yeah, aight."

"I'm serious. I'll put everything together, okay?"

"Heard you!"

"Sen?"

"What?"

"We're going to get back on track. I promise. I'm done with everything." I spoke.

"Yeah?" He asked chuckling, but I didn't find anything funny.

"What's so funny?"

"Nothing shorty. Nothing. Do ya thing ma."

"I'm serious. I don't want to lose you!" I admitted.

"We'll see. Only time will tell though." He said and walked out of the kitchen.

With Leland being gone and Tee screwing me over I just wanted to focus on my relationship with Sen. I was buggin' I wasn't sure if I wanted this relationship still. I didn't know up until last night that I wanted things to work between us. I know I cheated but this lick we were bout to hit was going to change our lives, and finally, the two of us could move on and focus on repairing our relationship.

Skylen

I was currently getting myself together preparing to walk out of the door, so I could hurry up and make it to work. I was running a little late this morning and , unfortunately, I wasn't going to be able to stop and get my usual hot chocolate. After Sen left last night a weird feeling came over me, and for the life of me I couldn't fall asleep. It had to be a little after three before I was finally able to shut my eyes which in return caused me to wake up late.

Grabbing my keys and purse, I locked up my apartment and hauled ass to my car. Ms. Jenn was sitting on her porch smoking a cigarette as usual, and like every other morning she waved at me, but this time she decided to speak.

"Hey, little Amish girl!" She said smirking.

"Huh?" I questioned.

"If you can huh you can hear missy. I called you

Amish!"

"Amish? But.. Nevermind I'm running late I gotta go!"

"I bet you are. I know what happened last night." She said and winked, and if I was white, I would have turned red in embarrassment.

Instead of responding I got into my car and drove like a bat out of hell to work. The whole ride there I kept trying to figure out how did she even find out! I know good, and damn well his black ass ain't tell his momma that he fucked me! If he did that was just corny and childish. Who brags about fucking someone nowadays?

I'm not ashamed of what I did. In fact, I didn't know what to feel. I mean Leland and I just broken up not too long ago and here I was poppin' coochie for a nigga I didn't even know. But God it felt so good. He catered to my love below. He frenched kissed her so passionately you would have thought his life depended on it.

Making it to work I quickly parked my car and

rushed inside to clock in. Once I made it to our work area, I walked straight to my cubicle but before I could put my things down my boss was walking towards me. Fuck! I was only fifteen minutes late. Eight if you minus the seven-minute grace period.

"Skylen, can you come to my office?" My boss asked me with a stern look on her face.

"Is everything okay? Am I in trouble?" I asked confused.

"Just come to my office. Bring your things with you."

"If you're firing me just get it over with now."

"My office, now please." She spoke before walking away, and I followed her before glancing at Lauren, and she just shrugged her shoulders.

Once we made it to her office, there were two police officers standing to the side engaging in small talk until they noticed us come in. Immediately I began to panic inside because one I hated the cops. For two what could they possibly want with me.

"Hi, are you Skylen Taylor?" The officer closer to me asked, and I shook my head yes.

"You may want to have a seat."

"I'm find where I am. What's going on?" I asked with a nervous chuckle.

"Uh, do you know a Leland Jacobs?"

"Yes, we uh we dated for a long time. Is he in some type of trouble?"

"I'm sorry, but Leland was shot yesterday and-"

"He was shot? Are you sure you have the right guy?"

"Ma'am." The second officer chimed in.

"We're sure it's the right guy. He was shot at a hotel."

"I'm not understanding. Is he okay? Why wouldn't he just call me and tell me himself?"

"Leland passed away. He was pronounced dead at the scene and we."

I didn't hear anything else that was said after they revealed that he was dead. Who would do this to him? He didn't bother anyone! I just don't understand how something like this could happen to him or why.

Before realizing what had happened, I released a gut-wrenching scream before falling to my knees. No. This couldn't be real life right now. This had to be a joke. That's it. This was a sick joke someone was playing on me. I refused to believe it.

"I'm sorry for your loss," the first officer said as he and his partner walked out.

I just saw him a week ago. This had to be wrong. There was no way that this was true. I was going to call his phone, and he was going to pick up, right? He had to. The moment he saw my name he would answer. I just know he will.

"Skylen, go home. Take all the time you need." My boss said walking out of the office while I remained on the floor crying from the depths of my soul.

Shortly after I could feel Lauren wrapping her

arms around me telling me, it will be okay, but I didn't want to hear that. Would it be okay? She couldn't understand or fathom the pain I was feeling. She couldn't even begin to understand.

"Let me take you home. Okay?" Lauren said helping me up, but I pulled away from her and stormed out of the building with tears running down my eyes.

I wasn't in the best condition to drive, but I needed to be alone. I wanted to be alone. I dialed his number back to back waiting for him to answer but all it did was go to his voicemail. He was gone. He was really gone.

Sen

"What's good brodie?" Grimey asked as soon as I got into his whip.

"Ain't shit. Thanks for picking me up." I told him.

"Wassup with you?"

"Mannn I can't call it. Just out here getting to this money."

"I hear you."

"Fuck going on with ya whip? You straight?"

"Need some work done. I need to grab a rental over on Boston Road. Think you can swing me by there?"

"Joint next to Walmart?"

"Yeah, that one."

"I was heading that way anyway." He spoke and

then the car was silent as he drove. That didn't last for long though.

"Aye, thanks for looking out. You did me a solid. Thirty bands ain't enough to repay you."

"It's cool. Just don't have me doing ya dirty work again ma'fucka. What the lil nigga do anyways?"

"Sis said he violated her on some forcing her to have sex with him type shit. You already know if a muthafucka violates her he disrespecting me. Ain't no hard feelings, but he had to go."

"Heard you."

"What's goin on wit you and that lil brown skin joint that stay next to ya mama crib?"

"Ain't shit going on with us," I told him and it was the truth. I smashed, but we weren't a couple or no shit like that. I was digging her lil cute ass though, but V was still very much in the picture.

"Nigga you lying like a muthafucka right now, you fucked, didn't you?" He asked taking his eyes off of the road and grinning, but I didn't say shit.

"Aight you don't have to confirm it, but I know my nigga, and I know you took down that pussy. Mr. Family man ain't so perfect after all huh?"

"You's a nosey bitch, you know that?" I asked chuckling.

"I was told if you want to know something ask nigga. My fault."

"Yeah aight. Yo ass just nosey. Always been. Goofy ass lookin' nigga."

"That's aight, I still get these bitches though. Everywhere I go these hoes call me handsome though." He boasted pulling up to the car rental place Enterprise.

"Thanks for the ride bro."

"Ah boy you know I got you. What you getting into later?"

"I don't know. Why? Sup?"

"Tryna hit the strip joint?"

"I don't know. Just hit me up and I'll hit you."

"Nigga it's Tuesday night you know the place bouta be flooded."

"I hear you. Just hit me up fam." I told him getting out the car and walking into the place.

***

"Sen, what we doing here? I thought we were going to dinner." Valencia said with an attitude.

I've been doing a lot of thinking about her and I relationship and her neglecting her child wasn't sitting right with me. I wanted her to see her. I wanted her to finally step up to the plate and remove the burden off her aunt. I'm as hood as it gets, but my one weakness is children. That little girl didn't deserve to be pawned off to her great aunt because her mother was a dumb ass bird and wanted to be a hoe.

"Get out," I spoke to her calmly.

"For what? Why the fuck are we here?"

"You heard what the fuck I said. Get out."

"I'm not goin no fuckin' where! The hell are we doing at my aunties house?!" She yelled irritating the fuck outta me.

"Answer me!"

"Bitch if you don't get yo ma'fuckin' ass out this fuckin car?! Act like you got some fuckin' sense and grow the fuck up. Now let's go!" I said raising my voice and getting out of the car.

I felt like I was talking to a fucking child. I was getting tired of her theatrics . I don't even know why I even kept trying knowing that shit between us been over since she came home with dick breath. Any other bitch would love to be in her position yet here I am trying to make shit work before I finally gave up.

When I made it to her aunts' front door, she realized I wasn't playing and finally got her ass out of the car. Seconds later a frail lady opened the door with a weak smile. You could tell she was an attractive woman, but with the bags under her eyes and sunken in cheeks, you could also tell that she was barely holding on. She looked tired.

"Michelle?" I asked, and she gave me a weak

smile.

"You must be Jensen. So nice to meet you." She greeted hugging me before looking over at Valencia.

"Hey Aunty." Valencia said with an attitude, and I shot her a look to let her know to get her shit together.

"Hey, Niecey. Why don't the two of you come on in." She welcomed and we all walked inside and into what looked like a dining room.

"How have you been pretty girl?"

"I've been okay."

"Are you here for Harmony? She's napping right now."

"What you telling me for? It was his idea to come here not mine!" She snapped, and I grabbed her by her arm and pulled her over by the front door.

"I don't know what the fuck the attitude is for but lose it. That's your fuckin' daughter you acting funky about. Act like you give a fuck with your sorry ass!"

"I didn't ask to come here!"

"Yeah? And I didn't ask to be with a fuckin' junky either." I hissed.

"Tighten the fuck up with your goofy ass."

"You don't understanddd." She whined, but I walked away from her and went to where her aunt was.

"Sorry about that," I apologized, but she fanned her hand.

"I'm used to it. It's been a long time I allowed her outbursts to affect me. I keep hoping that she'll come around, but it just seems to me that she keeps getting worse. I'm fighting as hard as I can for Harmony, but I'm tired." She confessed, and I saw it in her eyes that she was hurt by Valencia's actions.

"What is it that you need? What will give you a peace of mind?"

"Harmony being taken care of by a good family. That's all I want. I want her to be safe. I want her to be loved. I need her to go to a good home since that child in the other room don't want her."

"We will find her a home, okay?" I told her, and I meant it. I was going to do my very best to make sure that Michelle would be at peace and Harmony would be okay.

Skylen

It has been a few days since I found out about Leland's death and I was still having a hard time believing he was gone. I kept thinking he would call my phone begging to come home but that never happened. His death was being announced all on the news so much that I turned the TV off and hadn't turned it back on since. I just been laying in our bed as tears continuously fell from my eyes.

I kept blaming myself. If I hadn't ignored all his calls and just gave our relationship one more chance I wouldn't be going through this. Had I never kicked him out he would still be here. It was my fault, and nobody could tell me differently.

His mother called me a thousand times but I never answered. A few of his friends called, and still, I didn't answer. Lauren even called and popped up a few times, but I refused to answer. I didn't want to talk to anyone. I just wanted to be left alone. I was grieving, and nothing nobody says can make me feel better.

This feeling I was feeling was something I have never felt before. Not even him putting his hands on me hurt my heart as much as this shit does. What was I supposed to do now? How was I going to be able to cope without him? It feels like someone ripped my heart out of my chest and technically he did because despite everything he had my heart, and it'll never be the same.

They had no leads on who did this, and that wasn't a surprise. Niggas get killed every day out here, and most of the murders go unsolved. As much as I would love for them to find out who did this shit, I knew that they wouldn't so seeking closure from this would never happen. I will just have to deal with it.

For days I've laid here and reminisced about the good times we've had, and I just wish that we had a chance to go back to that. I wish that we could relive the moments again. At one point Le and I had a great relationship. We used to have fun and with him gone I didn't want to remember him with the bad memories. I wanted to remember the good times. For example, my twenty first birthday. He surprised me and took me to Atlantic City. That was the night I gave him my virginity, and I'll never forget it.

***

"Thank you," I smiled up at him while we walked hand in hand on the boardwalk.

"What you thanking me for beautiful?" He asked moving some hair out of my face.

It was a beautiful summer day. The weather wasn't too hot, maybe about in the middle eighties or something. There was a slight breeze seeing as though we were right next to the ocean and the sun was setting. It was beautiful. Almost like a scene out of a movie.

"For surprising me with this trip, thank you."

"It's no big deal. You deserve it."

"You're too good to me," I spoke causing his forehead to wrinkle in confusion as he looked down on me.

"Too good? What you mean?"

"*You do all the right things, yet I still haven't given you any.*"

"*Sky what you talkin' bout girl?*"

"*You know.. Like we haven't had sex. I've given you head and let you even get my booty, but that's as far as it goes with us.*"

"*I mean I know when you're ready you'll give it to me. I definitely would love for your first to be with me but I ain't going to pressure you.*" *He said, and then things got quiet between the both of us. Both letting our minds occupy us a bit.*

So many couples were out enjoying this beautiful weather. Some straight, some gay but they all the women held smiles like mine. I even saw one couple sitting on a bench, and although they were trying to be discreet, you can tell that he was fingering her. I guess they're spontaneous.

Then I saw the couples with kids, and that surely made me smile. I've always been on the fence when it comes to children. One day I want them, the next I don't. I often fantasized what children with Leland would be like. With him being well over six feet with caramel skin and dark eyes.

Me a tiny five feet even brown skinned and big doe eyes I wondered what kind of creation we would create.

Him squeezing my hand made me look at him before giving him a small smile. Tonight was the night. Tonight, I would give him my virginity. We've been together for a while, and we've done everything else. Why not give him my virginity? In my eyes, this was the perfect time.

Smiling, I told him "I'm getting chilly."

"Ready to go in?"

"Yeah, the wind is picking up, and I don't have any sleeves."

"Aight baby," He responding and with that, we went inside of The Tropicana where we were staying and went right up to our room.

"I'm going to shower, okay?" I told him, and he said okay.

In the shower I had everything mapped out with how it would happen. I played out different types of scenarios in my head, but they were all so corny and cheesy. I was nervous. I was officially about to become a woman. Who wouldn't be nervous?

Throwing my hair into a messy ponytail with a few strands of hair dangling on the side of my face. Oiling up my body nice and slowly, I sprayed some Jessica Simpson Fancy perfume before wrapping myself up in a clean plush towel. Walking out into our room, I walked over to where he was and stood directly in front of him.

"Skylen, what you doing?" He asked me looking up at me.

"I'm ready."

"Ready for what?"

"You know."

"Sky. Ready for what?"

"For you to take my virginity, Leland, duh! Let's do it!" I said irritated because he was acting so dumb.

"You sure?"

"If I wasn't I wouldn't have said it."

"Once we go there you can't take it back."

"Nigga who's the virgin here? You or me? You

acting more scared than me!"

"Ain't nobody scared, I'm just saying I don't want to hear shit after. You know you like to do stuff on impulse just to complain about it later."

"Well I don't want to think about the aftermath, I just want to do it. So you going to do it or what? We're doing everything else might as well do this too." I suggested and he didn't put up a fight. He gave in to everything I wanted. Happy Birthday to me!

***

Losing my virginity wasn't all that it was cracked up to be. It was painful, and he was off beat for all the two minutes that he lasted. It wasn't romantic at all. He even got a little bit of his sweat in my mouth, and I kid you not a bitch thought she was about to die.

But if I had to experience all of that all over again, I would. I would probably do a few things over, but if it meant having a little more time with Leland, I'd be all game.

"Sky!! I know you're in there! Open up!" I heard

Lauren yell as she banged on my window.

"If you don't open up I'm just going to call the police. It's been days Sky, open the damn door!"

Was this bitch serious? Talking about calling the cops. I was mourning, why couldn't she understand that? My nigga was killed. Never coming back again and all I wanted to do was be left the hell alone. But I also didn't want her to call the cops either. She knows I hated the police. So before her aggy ass calls the police, let me just get on up.

Walking to the door, I snatched the door open, and there she was standing there looking worried. Why? I don't know. If she thought I was going to do some dumb shit she had me all types of fucked up. Weak bitches pull stunts like that and I was far from weak, I was just hurting.

"Oh, My God! Sky I've been coming by and calling you for days!" She said hysterically throwing her arms around my neck.

"I'm fine Laur. I'm alive and well as you can see." I said rolling my eyes.

"Bitch please you look like shit, and you better not be rolling your eyes. You had me worried!"

"I'm fine though. You were worried for nothing."

"Girl bye! You're my best friend, if you're going through something so am I. I don't care if I didn't care for him, you did so let me be here for you!" She spoke pulling away from me, and instead of putting up a fight I simply turned around walking back into the house, and she followed.

Once we were inside, I sat on the couch while she sat on the loveseat. Together we just sat in silence. I didn't have much to say. In fact, I had absolutely nothing to say. I guess she understood because moments later she stood up and started cleaning my apartment. It wasn't all that messy, but it wasn't as spotless as I normally would keep it.

Instead of protesting I layed back on the couch and let my thoughts consume me again.

Sen

I had just pulled up to my momma's house when I caught myself staring over at Skylen's crib. I haven't spoken to baby since the night we slept together, and that was a lil second ago. I couldn't even call her because shorty never gave me her number. I ain't gon' sweat it though when she's ready she'll reach out to a nigga. They all do.

Gettin' out my whip I made my way inside of mom dukes crib where she was sitting in the living room watching the news. I never understood her reason for watching that shit. It was the same depressing shit every time you watched that ma'fucka. Taking a seat, I sat there silently until a commercial came on.

"Ma, can I ask you somethin'?"

"What Jensen?" She asked with her head cocked to the side as if I was bothering her.

"You ever think about leaving?"

"Leaving? Leaving where?"

"This shit hole? You never thought about relocating away from all of this bullshit?"

"I have, but this is home. Why? You thinking about leaving?"

"Yeah. But I don't know. Part of me want to go and start the fuck over somewhere else, but the other part has me feelin' like I'd be missin' something if I go." I told her as I rested each elbow on my knees.

"You got yourself in some trouble? That's the only time a person wants to up and leave and start over."

"Nah. Not sayin' it can't happen, but I stay under the radar for the most part. I just keep getting a funny feelin' bout shit."

"Then you need to stop your shit before your ass goes back to jail." She fussed.

"I ain't even out here doing nothing." I lied before quickly changing the subject.

"Valencia has a child that she doesn't take care of. I don't know how I feel about that deadbeat shit." I blurted, and my mother muted her tv and looked at me like a I was crazy.

"A child? Where the hell did she get a damn child from?"

"Ma."

"I'm just saying. I never knew the lil bitch had kids. You know I can't respect a woman who opened her legs, laid down made a child then abandoned the child."

"It's a girl. She's about twelve or some shit like that. She has down syndrome. Her aunt got custody but she dying. Valencia junky ass talking about she don't want the girl."

"And you being the man that you are feel like there's something you can do huh?"

"I mean yeah. But then the other part of me just feels like it ain't my place."

"That's because it ain't your place. I understand

you feeling like you want to do something but that ain't your problem nor is it your battle to fight. It's Valencia's. You pacify that girl too much." She spoke.

"What you mean?" I questioned.

"You enable her. As long as you continue to do that she'll never get it together. I thought you were thinking about leaving her."

"I was. I still am but I figured I'd give it one more try before I throw the towel in. We have some unfinished business right now, so I can't just leave."

"That girl is going to be your downfall. You just watch. I wish you'd find yourself a nice girl to settle down with. A girl like Skylen. I like her."

"Ma."

"Ma hell. You think I don't see that you've been coming by more often then you used to. You tryna see that girl. I know." She said with a grin on her face.

"I have no idea what you're talking about."

"Yeah okay. I'm old, not stupid. You like her

Jensen. It's okay. You crushing on the girl next door."

"Here you go. I'm bouta get out of here before you start scheming."

"Baby boy I don't need to scheme seems like you got it all covered. I know you slept with that girl."

"Yeah, it's definitely time for me to go." I tols her standing up.

"Ass in the hot seat and can't handle it."

"Nah, I just got some place I need to be."

"Mmmhmm. Whatever you say." She spoke, and I walked over to her and kissed her forehead and turned around to walk away. Before I was able to make it to the door, she spoke again.

"Be safe out there baby. You're all I have!"

"Always ma!" I yelled back at her then closing her door.

When I walked outside, I saw the chick Sky be with carrying a couple of bags. Looked like she had went shopping or something. Every time I came this way shorty car was parked in the same spot as if she hadn't been leaving the house.

"Aye," I yelled to the girl.

"Yes?" She asked surprised that I was talking to her.

"She good? I haven't seen her in a while."

"She's been better. Her boyfriend was killed. She's just trying to deal with it." She responded and continued on to what she was doing.

Damn. I had no idea the pussy ass nigga was dead. If you asked me, he didn't deserve her sympathy, but I understood. From what she's told me they were together for a while, so it's only right for her to be emotional. Fuck it. I'll see her when I see her.

***

"You ready?" I asked Valencia as I leaned against the door frame of our bedroom.

"I guess." She said before picking at her nails.

"Wassup wit you? You aight?"

"I keep getting this nagging feeling in my stomach. Maybe we should abort this mission."

"Nah, you wanted to do this, and you wanted to do it your own way, so I'm letting you."

"I'm tellin' you Sen I just don't feel right. I'm going to tell him I had an emergency or something."

"You serious right now V?"

"Sen, please trust me on this. Please. Let'a give it a few days." She begged and pleaded with her eyes.

"Aight man. We can wait. Since you putting a pause right now, I'm bouta go holla at Grimey real quick, aight?" I told her and by the look on her face she wanted to protest, but she didn't. She just dropped her head. Without speaking another word, I grabbed my keys and left.

Valencia

I'm not sure what's wrong with me, but I just had a weird feeling. I can't really explain it, but my stomach was in knots. I was supposed to be going out with Tee tonight, but something was off. What? Can't tell you that because I don't know so here I was waiting on him to pick up the other end of the phone. After a couple of more seconds, his deep voice answered.

"Yo."

"Hey," I said softly.

"Wassup girl? You almost done?" He asked and I could tell that he was smoking by the sound of his voice.

"No, you think we can reschedule?"

"For what?"

"I have a family emergency with my aunt that I need to take care of." I lied chewing on my bottom lip.

"Yeah, aight. Stop wasting my time ma."

"How am I wasting your time if something came up with my aunt? I'll make it up to you, I just want to make sure she's okay."

"Heard you. I'll hit you back. Matter of fact you hit me up when you're done playing games." He said and hung up on me.

Rude ass Hartford niggas. I swear I can't stand them. He acting like he really gave a fuck when he didn't. Sorry no dick having ass just wanted to fuck. He thought he was using me, but I was using him. I just wanted his money. Nothing more. Nothing less.

I just needed to cook up a different plan. One less risky. I know he's supposed to head out of town in a few days so maybe I can just go to his house and take what I can. I'm just not in the mood to fake the funk with anyone right now. Especially him.

Getting up, I walked into our spare bedroom and into the small walk in closet. Removing a box from out of the very back, I sat on the floor indian style as I opened it. It's been years since I went through this box. So many memories I wished to bury.

Opening it up I grabbed the folded up piece of paper that had my daughters info on it and just stared down at it. It was her birth certificate. I also had baby photos and cards that I never got around to sending in this box.

See Sen and my aunt thought that I was just a deadbeat momma, but I wasn't. In the summer time I go to the day program she goes to and just watch her when they take her outside. I have pictures of her all throughout her childhood, but I just couldn't be a mother to her. She deserved more than me. Which was why I gave her up.

Yes, she is a product of rape technically however, I'm not as heartless as I may come off. I knew the whole time I was carrying her I wasn't going to be able to raise her. There was absolutely no way that I would be able to look in her face for the rest of her life see him in her and not resent her. If I had it my way I would have aborted her. But my poor excuse of a momma refused to sign for it, so I ended up having her.

Still, with auntie Michelle dying, I couldn't bring

myself to raise her. I was selfless enough to not want to take on that responsibility and put her in a horrible situation. I just wished Sen and Michelle understood that. I was tired of them trying to force me to take her.

I'm a fucked up individual. This I know but don't judge me because I'm sure you got your own set of problems. None of us are perfect so if you're looking down on me like your shit don't stink fuck you.

Continuing to go through the box I came across a photo of my younger self. Mom had did my makeup, making me look pretty. She even did my hair, had me thinking we were going to have a mommy daughter day. But the truth was she dressed me up just to sell me for a fuckin' rock. Can you believe that?

* **

"Valenciaaaaaaaa!" I heard my momma yell my name while I was in my bedroom listening to my B2K cd.

"Huhhhhh?!" I yelled back waiting for her to say something, but she didn't so I got up and walked into her bedroom where I saw her messing with her makeup.

"Yes, ma?"

"Want to play dress up? Want mommy to make you more beautiful?"

"How?"

"I'm going to do your makeup. Come have seat baby." She said gesturing for me to have a seat on her bed.

I had just turned twelve so her tellin me she wanted to do my makeup had me feeling myself. Not asking any questions I sat there for about twenty minutes before she started on my hair. Once she was done, she looked at me and smiled wide.

"What's wrong?" I asked her scared.

"Nothing. You look beautiful. Go look in the mirror. " She told me, and I did that, and she was right. I really did look nice. She might be a drunk but she definitely knew how to keep herself up.

"Valencia, I'm having company. Go shower and put something pretty on. Just don't mess up your hair."

"Okay."

After about thirty minutes or so the company she said

she was having came, and it was a tall skinny light-skinned man with a scar in the middle of his forehead. He wasn't bad looking. He actually was kinda cute, but he kept looking at me like I was his favorite meal.

Little did I know tonight would change my life forever.

***

I lost my virginity that day. I never told anyone, but I believe a piece of my soul was lost that day as well. I haven't been the same since.

Skylen

A Few Days Later

Today was the day. I've been dreading this day all week. As I stood outside the massive church, I couldn't bring myself to move. My anxiety was getting the best of me, and I was feeling an attack coming on soon. I knew today was coming, but I didn't think it would come so quick.

"Hey," Lauren whispered squeezing my hand.

"I got you. We don't have to stay just pay your respects and go."

"Lauren, I don't think I can do this. This shit ain't fair. I shouldn't be here right now." I said through a shaky voice.

"You're right. It isn't fair, but life is never fair. We just have to roll with the punches. I'm here. I got you."

She was right life isn't fair, and right now I hated God for taking Leland away. We're only twenty-six. We shouldn't be burying either one of us, but here I was preparing to say goodbye to the man I've spent the last eight, nine years with.

Finally building up the courage the both of us walked into the church hand in hand. It was packed. Service hadn't started yet, and people were still viewing the body. As bad as I didn't want to walk up there I had to. I had to see his face one last time. I needed to kiss his lips one last time.

Every step I took I could feel all eyes on me which made me uncomfortable. I never enjoyed having all eyes on me, but today there was nothing I could do about it. In my fitted black dress, I had picked up from Forever 21 and my black Jessica Simpson heels. I solemnly made my way with my bestie by my side to the altar where Leland lay in the casket. The closer I got, the more I could see him, and every step was beginning to get a little harder than the last.

Once I made it to his casket, I looked down into

his face, and he didn't even look the same. He didn't look like my boyfriend. He looked.. he looked deformed. Whoever was responsible for the preparation of his body did the best that they could, but my baby didn't look the same. Taking my hand, I placed it on top of his while I laid my head on his chest and just cried. I released the loudest gut-wrenching scream and just cried.

The saying 'You never know what you have until it's gone' is right. I never understood it until this very moment. My heart ached. It was broken. Someone selfishly took him away from me and didn't even care. They didn't think about the pain they would cause the people who loved him. They didn't care. I don't know what Leland could have possibly done to get himself killed, but I can guarantee that he didn't deserve this.

Standing up after a few minutes with tears still falling from my eyes I leaned into him and kissed his cold lips before whispering into his ear.

"I'm sorry. I'm so sorry. I love you Lelandddd. I love youuuu!" I said through tears before I finally gotten the strength to walk, but that didn't last long because as soon as I took a step, my knees buckled.

"Skylen baby! Joe help her!" I heard Leland's mother say to his father and he did. With him and Lauren, they walked me to a seat right behind he and his wife.

This was really happening. I was really saying goodbye to him. Everything felt so surreal and life as I know it has changed in a blink of an eye. Life will never be the same for me after this. I could feel it. I would never be able to get over his death.

As the pastor went over the order of the service, I just sat there spaced out not really listening. He was going on and on about how great of a boy Leland was all while sending his condolences to everyone grieving. Scanning the crowd, I spotted Valencia. That was odd. What was she doing here? I had no idea the two of them knew one another.

Not wanting to give things too much thought I turned my attention back to the pastor and then the church choir started singing. Thank god because I was tired of hearing him repeat himself. He didn't know Leland. That was obvious by his speech, and I was over it.

Why do you cry? He has risen. Why are you weeping? He's not dead. Why do you cry? He has risen. Why are you weeping? He's not dead. He paid it all on that lonely highway, and his anointing I can feel. He shed his blood, for my transgressions and by his stripes, we are healed.

The choir sounded beautiful. Their voices were amazing. But that didn't change the fact that he wasn't coming back. That this was the last time, I would ever see him.

***

"How are you holding up baby?" Leland's mom Clara asked me smiling. Her eyes weren't filled with the same twinkle it once held. Her smile seemed forced nonetheless she wanted to see how I was doing.

"I'm okay mama. How are you? Do you need anything?"

"Oh no, I got my Jesus and Joe that makes sure I'm alright. I never expected something like this to happen, but it did. I'm still processing it. But you, you're alone. Who's there for you? I know how much the two of you mean to one another."

"I'll be fine. I promise." I told her just as I spotted Valencia.

"Will you be at the repast?"

"I'm not sure. If I don't make it, I promise to come by and see you, okay?"

"Okay baby." She replied giving me a hug and kiss on the cheek before walking away.

Walking over to Lauren's car I saw Valencia walk to the car parked next to us in a hurry, so I put a little pep in my step and caught her just in time before she was able to get her body completely into the car.

"Valencia!" I called, and she looked in my direction.

"Skylen?" She questioned, and I walked up to her while Lauren blew her horn.

Sticking my finger up I signaled for her to give me a minute. When I made it to Valencia, she looked stressed. Worried kind of. You can tell that she had been crying.

"What are you doing here? I didn't know you knew my boyfriend."

"Leland?"

"Uh yeah. That's why everyone is here. How did you know him?" I asked, and she fidgeted with her hands for a bit before responding.

"I don't know him. I used to go to the same gym as him. Just thought I'd pay my respects. I really got to get going though; I'm kinda in a rush." She said, and I just nodded my head as she jumped in her car and pulled off.

That was weird.

Sen

"Nigga where the fuck we going?" I asked Grimey as he drove up Bay street.

"Wanna show you somethin'. Think this shit is right up ya alley."

"Fuck you talkin' bout bro?"

"Muthafucka calm yo ass down and let me show you." He fired back smoking a blunt.

"Fuck you think you talkin' too nigga? I ain't yo bitch!"

"You nigga. You askin questions like you my bitch!"

"Yeah aight pussy. Just watch yo fuckin' tone!"

"Aight my bad bitch. Your ass been on edge like a ma'fucka lately. You aight?" He asked changing his tone.

"I'm smooth."

"It's that fine lil bitch huh?"

"What?" I asked confused.

"Shorty that stay next to ya moms."

"Oh nah, I haven't spoken to her."

"Nigga you fucked and got curved? You let a bitch hoe you?"

"Fuck outta here. You know it ain't even that type of time goofy."

"You know you just admitted to fuckin' her, right?" He asked laughing, but I waved him off and just sat back into the seat.

Noticing we were out here in Longmeadow, I looked at him like he was crazy. Wasn't shit out here but white muthafuckas. Fuck was he doing out here with their weird asses?

"You see that house right there?" He pointed to the white house with a white fence around it.

"What about it?"

"Money in there. Lots of it and I want it. Catch

my drift?"

"Yeah? How you know?"

"Fuckin' this lil white bitch. Bitch nasty as fuck too, but her father is some nigga with a mean coke habit. He's been on some fluke shit with me, and I want my money."

"Who all stay in the house?"

"Just him. Wife died a few years ago in a car accident. The girl comes home on the weekends. I served him few a months back and stumbled across her during one of my transactions. Anyways he thought shit was smooth because he found out I was taking his hoe ass daughter down and felt like he could rip me off. Sent the money through her the last time and it wasn't adding up. Been tryna reach his ass but he dodging me."

"So, what this gotta do with me?"

"Need you to help me go in this bitch and take it. He's alone. Shit should be easy, I just needed a little reinforcement behind me that's all."

"So, what makes you think he got money just laying around in the house?"

"His daughter told me. He keeps an emergency stash in the freezer. Ain't shit to get it."

"And the girl? Fuck you gon do wit her?"

"Nothing. She ain't a threat. Her ass was so high when she was ranting the other night she probably don't even remember tellin' me all of his shit." He grinned.

"You a grimey ma'fucka, you know that right?" I asked laughing.

"I know. You coming or what?"

"Ma'fucka does it look like I got a choice. In and out bro. Mad crackas out here we need to do this shit fast and be out."

"Of course. You strapped?"

"Of course."

"Say less. Let's go." He said, and the two of us got out of the car and jogged up to the house.

It was quiet. The sun had just gone down, so people were just getting home. Probably from work and they were unaware of what was about to happen. I watched Grimey as he casually walked up to the man's front door and knocked as if it was a pleasant visit.

Once the man opened the door, he looked as if he could just shit on himself. Barging in Grimey looked around the house as if he was in awe. House was beautiful with marble floors, but we ain't have time to fraternize. Nah that's how ma'fuckas got caught up.

"Dope ass home you got here Bill," Grimey spoke smiling.

"T-t-t-thank you." The man stuttered over his words.

"You mind if my friend and I take a seat?"

"N-n-no."

"Calm down buddy, no need to be nervous."

"Why, why are you here?"

"We have a problem," Grimey told him while motioning with his head in the direction of the kitchen.

While I walked away and into the kitchen, I slipped on a glove and opened the fridge. Wasn't hard for me to find what I was looking for because wasn't shit in the freezer but a couple of plastic containers. Removing them, I popped opened the lids, and the girl was right. There was money inside in a Ziploc bag. Grabbing everything I walked back out into the living room.

"You know Bill, I actually liked you, and I hate that I even have to do this to you."

"You, you you don't have to. I have your money, just let me go get it. It's in my bedroom." He said nervously.

"Where in the bedroom?"

"In the heating vent. Take it all!"

"Handle that." Grimey said to me, and I made my way up the stairs making sure not to touch anything.

When I got into the bedroom, I saw the vent immediately. Before touching it, I slipped on the other glove. I know you're probably wondering what I was doing with gloves in my pocket randomly. In the business I'm in, I never know when I'll hit a lick. You see the stunt this nigga pulled, right? Spontaneous shit. I had to always be ready. I've been doing this a long time without being caught, and I needed shit to stay that way. I'd die before a nigga went back to jail.

Walking over to the vent, I opened it, and there was a manila envelope. Grabbing it, I opened it and like he said there was money inside. Fingering a few bills, there was nothing but a bunch of Ben Franks. Leaving out the room I was making my way down the stairs when I heard a shot fired.

"Nigga, you couldn't wait?" I asked when I made it down the stairs.

"I heard you ass coming down. Let's get out of here!" He said, and we rushed out the house.

This nigga was sloppy.

Valencia

After pondering about a few things, I decided to go talk to my aunt and see Harmony. I know the last time didn't go too well, so I wasn't too sure how things were about to go. I've been holding on to so much hurt over the years that it caused me to be this bitter person that I didn't like. So here I was sitting outside my aunt's house in my car trying to gather my thoughts.

I didn't know what I was going to say to my aunt. However, I think she deserved a conversation. I owed her that much. I didn't want her to think I was running away from my responsibility just for the fuck of it. I needed to explain to her that I just couldn't do it. Harmony is a reminder of my childhood. The childhood I've tried so hard to forget about.

Before getting out of the car my phone rang. It was Tee. After the last date didn't happen, he was mad, but I promised that I would make it up to him the next time. So, once I finished up everything here, I was going to meet him at the Holiday Inn Express near the airport.

"Hello," I spoke into the phone.

"We still on for later, right?" He asked me.

"Yeah, why do we have to meet at the hotel though?"

"It's just easier that way. Instead of having you drive all the way out here I rather us just meet in the middle."

"Okay, guess that makes sense."

"What's wrong with you? You don't trust me?"

"I'm not saying that. I was just curious. That's all."

"Want me to get you anything?" He asked, and I knew exactly what he was referring to.

Tee knew about my coke habit. He didn't judge me. He let me do me without judging, and maybe that's why I was diggin him so tough. Well until he kinda one nighted me until he felt as though I was convenient enough for him. A nigga like him had a plethora of hoes. So me, although I was beautiful was just another bitch under his belt.

"No, just something to drink," I told him looking at the time.

"I should be there in a hour or so, just send me the room info. Okay?"

"Got you." Was all he said before hanging up.

Taking a deep breath, I emerged from my car and took the short walk to her door. She must've been watching me because she opened it as soon as I reached the door. Instead of greeting me she walked away.

"I know I'm the last person you want to see." I started off saying when I locked eyes with her.

"Sit down Valencia." She spoke calmly. She looked tired. She looked worse than she did the last time Sen and I were here.

Doing as I was told, I took a seat in one of the recliners she had in her sitting area. For a while, we just looked at one another. Both emotional. This was the woman who took me in when her sister didn't want me, and I had been giving her my ass to kiss. I should have been thanking her, but I didn't. I never thanked her, and that realization is the very reason I was sitting here with tears falling from my eyes.

"I'm sorry." I apologized through tears.

"It's not your fault. I just want you to get it together Valencia. If not for yourself but for the little girl in the other room. Do it for her." She pleaded, but I shook my head no.

"You don't understand,"

"What don't I understand? Please tell me because there's no excuse for you to turn your back on your child. You're turning out to be her. You know that, don't you?"

"I've never wanted her. I can't look at her for the rest of my life and not think about how she was conceived. I can't do that!"

"Look, I know it isn't easy, but that's still your blood. She's still a part of you. Baby, I'm dying. I don't have that much more time left. I need you to be there for this girl. You're better than Monica. Your past does not define you. What happened to you as a child does not define the woman you are determined to be if you don't let it. You're repeating a cycle. Break it." She spoke with watery eyes.

"I'm just asking that you spend some time with her. Maybe after that, you'll have a different opinion."

"Auntie.. I can't. That man.." I sobbed.

"That man is long gone, sweetie. You need to let it go. You need to start healing. You on drugs just like ya momma. Don't let her decisions rub off on you."

"I don't know how to be a mother. I wouldn't know how to take care of her."

"You take care of her the way a mother should. You'll love her the way she should be loved. Love her the way I love you. You're not biologically mine, but I've taken care of you your whole life. I'm begging you just try. Please."

" I can-"

"Harmony! Harmony baby girl come here for a second." She called out to my daughter before standing up. After a couple of minutes, she came from the back of the house and joined us in the sitting room.

"Harmony, this is Valencia."

"Hi," she said quickly before walking over to my aunt taking a seat next to her.

"Hello, Harmony," I said through tears smiling.

As horrible as this is about to sound, I never met her. I've seen her from a distance but the last time I've been this close to my daughter was the day I pushed her out. She was always in the hospital for something when she was a baby, so I had no reason to interact with her. Not to mention she was Michelle's responsibility, not mines, so I moved out as soon as I was able to.

"You're pretty." She told me, and I smiled.

"I think you're the pretty one," I spoke back, and I wasn't lying. She looked a lot like me just a little different.

Sitting here across from her had so many emotions swirling around inside of me. I said I didn't want her, but for some reason the more I looked at her, the more I wanted to do better. I wanted to be better.

Skylen

"What are you doing here?" I asked Sen as he stood at my door.

"Wanted to check on you."

"This late? It's after midnight. What do you want?"

"You mad at a nigga?" He asked sounding stupid as hell.

"Did you just ask me that?"

"Yeah."

"You fucked me, and I haven't heard from you since. What you think?" I asked with an attitude.

"It ain't even like that. I heard what happened to your boyfriend. I wanted to give you your space. How you been holding up?"

"I'm okay."

"You're not okay Skylen. You have bags and shit

under your eyes. You ain't okay."

"What's it to you? Why do you care?"

"Because contrary to what you believe I care about you."

"You care about me, but you fucked and dipped? Right."

"I told you wasn't like that. I just came by to make sure you was good. That's all." He said turning and walking away.

I liked Sen., But I wasn't going to let him handle me the way he wanted to. I was going through enough with Leland passing, and I just wasn't trying to add on more than I could mentally and emotionally handle. Yet as he walked away I craved him. Crazy, right? I wanted him near me even if we didn't speak. I just wanted him close.

"Sen!" I yelled, and he turned around.

"Don't leave," I told him, and he didn't. He just stood there looking confused.

"Please. Just stay." I begged before walking away and sitting on the sofa.

I was hoping he would come in. If he doesn't walk through that door in five minutes that was cool, but I left my door wide open as the cold air made its way into my apartment in hopes that he would come in and he did. I didn't have to turn around to know that he was standing at the door, I could feel him. And when he took a seat next to me, I exhaled.

For a while, we sat and watched TV. I was watching this show on Lifetime called Married at First Sight. These people were crazy, but I tipped my imaginary hat off to them for being able to do something so drastic.

Can you imagine marrying a complete stranger and deciding after eight weeks if that marriage was what you wanted? I couldn't although I understood how some of these couples were able to grow to love someone in such a short time because I've grown pretty fond of Sen. I wasn't in love with him, but I was definitely smitten.

"Talk to me," he said breaking our silence.

"About?" I questioned clearing my throat.

"What's going on. How do you really feel?"

"I.. I don't know. It doesn't seem real. I saw him laying in that casket, but I just feel like I'm stuck in a nightmare that I can't wake up out of. I don't know. I want to be angry. I want to be able to mourn, but it's like I won't allow myself to."

"When was the last time you spoke to him? You know before all this shit happened?"

"The day you and him, got into that fight. I ignored his calls. He came by, and I wouldn't let him in. I just feel like if I would have forgiven him maybe he would still be here but.."

"But what?"

"Then you wouldn't be here," I told him honestly. I was conflicted. I'm mourning my boyfriend well ex-boyfriend meanwhile wanting the man that dissed me for weeks.

"Damn," he said lowly before running his hands over his waves.

"Sen, make me feel good. Please."

"Sky."

"Please."

"Sky you ain't thinking clearly right now."

"Sen, please. I need this." I begged, but he wouldn't budge. In fact, he wouldn't look at me. He was staring straight ahead at the TV.

Is it crazy of me to wanted to have sex with a man after burying my ex? Is it crazy that the only thing that would make me feel wanted by a man was sex right now? I was probably a little buzzed at this moment, but I just wanted him to fuck me like he did before. I wanted him to fuck me so hard and deep to the point that I wouldn't be able to walk in the morning. I just wanted him to take my mind off everything. I wanted to escape my reality even if it was for ten minutes.

I went from not wanting to be bothered with

him to not wanting him to leave. I went from talking about Leland to wanting to feel Sen deep inside of me. I was a raging ball of emotions and had no idea what to do with them. The more I sat next to him and him not acknowledging me the more rejected I started to feel. I stood up to leave, but he pulled me down on top of him.

I wasted no time attacking his sexy full lips. As I kissed him, I moaned. His lips were so soft and juicy and felt so amazing against mine. Never pulling our lips apart I helped him out of the shirt he was wearing. Finally stopping for some air, I bit down on my lip as I grinded into him. This little coochie of mine was hot, and it only wanted him.

Standing up I slowly undressed from head to toe as I watched him do the same. When I was done, he was sitting there with his big fat dick in his hand stroking himself. I wasted no time dropping to my knees and putting him into my mouth. I was trippin' for putting his dick in my mouth, but it looked so fucking good that I couldn't resist.

Swirling my tongue around the head, I sucked on it for a bit before inching him down my throat until it disappeared. Yeah, I knew all of the tricks when it came to giving oral. I lost my virginity late but sucking dick? I've been doing it since you know who and I started dating so I guess you could say I was a pro.

Tightening my throat muscles as I deep throated him I could hear low groans escape his lips making me smile inwardly. I could have easily made him cum off my head alone, but I didn't want that so I slowed down my pace and sucked him nice and slowly before pulling it out of my mouth making that popping sound.

His dick was beautiful. Perfect shaped mushroom head, perfect size, and girth. I loved it. Not to mention my kitty cat was purring because she knew what was ahead for her. Rubbing his dick on my lips for a bit, I stopped before straddling him.

I should've told him to use a condom but all common sense went out the window. I was hungry for him. For his dick and as he looked at me, he was hungry for me as well. With my hands planted on the back of the couch, I bounced up and down on him with my eyes closed tightly. His hands resting comfortably on my ass he helped guide me, and my head fell back in ecstasy.

"Fuuuuckkkkkkkk!" I cried.

"This shit feels so fuckin' proper. Fuck meeeeee!"

"Damn girl." He groaned still neither one of us stopped or slowed down our pace.

"Shit! You feel so good, oh you feel so fucking good!"

Compared to our first sex session this was filled with so much intensity. Everything that I have been feeling I was taking out on him while we fucked one another. I was talking to him without talking to him if you get what I'm saying. Biting down on his shoulder I started slowing down a bit. I didn't want it to end. I didn't want it to ever end.

Taking this as an opportunity he slapped me on my ass and told me to get on the floor. Doing as I was told I laid on the floor on my back. Spreading my pussy lips, I played in my wetness for him to see exactly how much my body responded to him. For a while, he sat and watched before he rammed his dick up in me making me flinch.

It hurt for that second but the more he stroked me, the more it felt good. The last time I thought I was going to pass out from his dick beating but this time around I was taking it like a fucking champ. You hear me? Your girl was fucking Sen back. I was matching his thrusts.

While he slid in and out of my pussy, I pinched my nipples with one hand while the other massaged my clit. My body couldn't take so much pleasure all at once because all of a sudden, the bottom of my stomach began cramping and I got the urge to pee. I was getting ready to cum, but I wasn't ready yet. I wanted him to cum with me.

"Seeeennnn, cum for me. Fuuuuuckkkk cum for me!" I moaned loudly as he his strokes became faster and harder.

He was pounding into me with so much force I

just knew that my pussy was going to be sore in the morning. I didn't mind one bit though. If you ask me this shit was well worth it.

"Fuck!" He grunted, and within seconds we both came together.

After thirty seconds or so he collapsed to the side of me while trying to get his breathing under control. Meanwhile, I just layed there and stared at the ceiling. This nigga made my fuckin' cervix smile, and my lil pussy was happier than a bitch too. Sore but happy nonetheless.

"Leaving?" I asked him never turning to look at him.

"You want me to?"

"Can I be honest?"

"Speak ya peace."

"No. No, I don't want you to leave, but you have someone else waiting for you so-"

"We ain't talkin' bout her. I asked you a question.

We talkin' bout me and you." He interrupted, and I turned to look at him.

"Stay with me for the night. Please." I spoke softly, and instead of responding he pulled me into him and held me.

I was lonely. Mourning the loss of my man. He had his own situation going on. I wasn't sure what the details were with him and Valencia and didn't care. I just wanted to enjoy him, even if it was only for tonight.

Valencia

I had just gotten back from spending two days with Tee, and my mind was officially made up. I was robbing him as soon as I was able to reach Sen. This is my last lick. The only reason I was going through with it because one, he's out of town. Two because he likes to brag and walk around like he's Nino Brown, so I just felt like I needed to knock him off his high horse. He thought because he had some money or whatever that it gave him the right to treat and talk to women like shit.

At first, my dumbass was feeling the nigga, but the more I get to know him the more I'm just disgusted with myself for even giving him the time of day. His no dick having ass had a lot of nerves to act the way he did. Nigga could barely eat pussy but wanted to be cocky as hell. Nope. I wasn't here for it.

After this though, I'm turning a new leaf. I wasn't completely sold on the idea of taking care of Harmony, but I cared enough to try. I promised myself if this lick goes smoothly, which it will that I will do whatever's necessary to provide for her and I meant it. My talk with my aunt touched me. Maybe because I went over there with a sober mind, who knows but I realized she was right.

I even kinda wanted to end things with Sen. I love him. He's all I know, but I need to heal from old wounds. I need to learn how to love myself and get my shit together. I know he would help if I let him, but it isn't his job to fix me. I just wanted him to support and respect my wishes.

Yeah, the two of us have history, but it isn't fair if either one of us stay in a relationship that's no longer feeding us. I don't know what the future holds but I do know that everything happens for a reason, I just hoped that when him and I had our conversation, he would be cool.

Skylen has crossed my mind as well a few times. I no longer had the desire to rebuild a friendship with her. After her revealing to me that Leland was indeed her boyfriend at the funeral, I couldn't stand to look at her. I was fucking him not knowing they were together. Not to mention had I not told him to meet me at the fucking hotel he would still be alive. He was killed while the two of us had sex. I will never be able to look her in her eyes again.

I may be a piece of shit, but I wouldn't do an innocent person like that. I wouldn't try to establish a relationship with them knowing I fucked their man. I'm shady, but a bitch does have morals.

***

All I got is these broken clocks, I ain't got no time just burning daylight. Still, love, and it's still love, and it's still love. It's still love, still love (still loving), still love.

I was in the kitchen frying some catfish with my baked mac and cheese in the oven and my cabbage in the pot cooking while I sung along to Sza. Sen wasn't home, he was out doing whatever it is he was doing, but I wanted to cook. I haven't been sniffin' as much, so I was sober more often, and I kind of enjoyed it.

I had a clearer mind, and I figured I could cook

some dinner, so Sen and I could talk about our relationship. I knew he was dealing with someone. The way we had sex changed up a bit. He didn't touch me the same. He didn't look at me the same, and it's been that way for some time now.

We were holding on to what used to be rather than paying attention to the layout in front of us. I wasn't even mad that he was seeing someone else. I figured it was a matter of time before he did anyway. With all of the fucked up shit, I've been doing behind his back I couldn't get mad. I had no room to.

"What you in here cooking?" I heard him ask me causing me to turn around.

"When you get here?"

"Just walked through the door. What you cooking for?"

"I was in the mood to cook. Hungry?"

"Yeah, lemme shower."

"Okay. Hurry so I can talk to you."

"Talk to me bout what? You aight?" He asked.

"Yeah, uh just go take your shower, and I'll fix our plates," I told him, and for a second, he just stood there looking at me until he finally turned and walked away. I hated when he did that. Every time he looked at me with those dark eyes I got nervous.

Preparing myself for our talk, I made our plates and sat them on the table. After that I grabbed some glasses filling them up with ice before pouring some lemonade in both cups. Putting the rest of the food up, I busied myself until he was sitting at the dinner table. I watched as he took a bite of the bake mac and cheese before looking up at me and smiling.

I knew I still had it. I probably don't cross you as a domestic woman, but Michelle raised me right. I just chose to do wrong. She taught me everything I needed to know to be a woman, but I was too busy trying to live the fast life. Still, somehow, I managed to remember some skills she had taught me.

"So talk.." He said never looking at me.

"I was thinkin.. I'm ready to hit Tee."

"Why now?"

"It just seems perfect. He's out of town. It'll be as easy as counting to three."

"And you know that for sure?"

"Yes, Sen. You trust me, right?"

"Is that a trick question?" He asked this time looking dead at me making me uncomfortable.

"Anyways after we hit this lick I'm done. For real this time. I went by my aunt's house and visited Harmony." I revealed looking up at him, and his face held a blank expression.

"I thought about how I showed my ass the last time and didn't like it, so I went over there to talk. She really wants me to take care of her. I don't know if I can do that."

"Valencia what are you scared of?"

"Huh?"

"What are you scared of? What's stopping you from stepping up and taking care of your responsibilities?"

"I.. I.. I don't know. She has down syndrome. How the fuck am I supposed to take care of a disabled child?"

"The same way you would take care of a normal child. She has a disability, not a fucking disease. You in your way. You might be good at this mother shit. Who knows." He said, and that kinda made me smile because he meant it.

"It's just so scary. I guess I think I'm going to fuck it up somehow."

"I mean life is all about fuck ups, but eventually you learn from them. Do what you gotta do V and stop making excuses."

"I hear you Sen. Trust me I hear you," I spoke to him, and I did hear him. I heard and understood him loud and clear.

Sen

"So when you thinking about doing this thing?" I asked V as I bit into my piece of catfish.

"Tonight."

"Tonight? What's the rush?"

"I don't want to take any chances. The sooner we get it done the better."

"Mannn I don't know about this."

"Come on Sen everything is going to be fine."

"Valencia, we usually plan hits out. You tryna act off impulse. This is how muthafuckas get murked or bagged. I ain't tryna get either."

"Sen, listen to me. I know where he lives. He lives in the cut. It'll be so easy. He so flashy and stupid he wouldn't suspect me at all. This shit could come from anybody." She said trying to persuade me, but I wasn't feeling it.

I was far from a pussy ass nigga, but I wasn't with impulsive shit. See that shit with Grimey? Impulsive and sloppy as fuck. That's not how I do business. Now here comes Valencia trying to cook a quick scheme not really thinking shit through. It can be a setup, and her dumb ass is falling for it, or he can very much so be out of town. Did I want to chance it? Nah. Would I have her back? Absolutely.

"Look if you tryna do this shit then let's do it. We can get this shit done around 4 am. Cool?" I asked her going against my better judgment.

Looking at my watch, the clock read 8:30 pm. I really didn't want to do this shit. Something wasn't right. I could very well be paranoid, but something doesn't seem right. It's like something is bouta happen, but I don't know what.

Finishing up my food I told Valencia I'd be back around midnight, so we can get this shit done and over with. Grabbing my keys, I jumped in my whip. Starting the ignition Meek Mill's song Dangerous was playing.

It was nights like this, feeling right like this. I never

really spent no time like this, huh. The second time at the crib knowing I might not hit, you said. "What I look like?" yeah. Look into your eyes, shit is dangerous. The pussy wet, I call it angel dust.

As the song played, I couldn't help but to think about Skylen. Whoever said opposites attract was right because a nigga like me didn't need a bitch with a college degree. She was a square, to say the least. Probably come from a good home or something yet she was fucking around with my kind.

I can't deny that I'm attracted to her, but I also can't be all up on her either as much as I would like. Valencia and I may not be rocking as tough with one another, however, shorty still my girl, so I can't give Sky all of me. To be honest, I don't even know if I want to. She didn't need me coming into her life fucking shit up. As much bad shit I've done it's only a matter of time before Karma has its way with me.

I probably shouldn't even be thinking like that but shit it is what it is. I ain't afraid of death. Every time I did what I did not making it back home always crossed my mind. Once you accept that death happens, it can't be prevented you start embracing that shit. So with all the shit that I do, I would hate to drag Sky into my mess.

It's just so fucking hard not to. When I was around shorty shit just flowed. She didn't want anything from me, she wasn't tryna make things into more than what they were, and I liked that. Things were easy with her.

Making it to my destination, I cut the car off and just sat in silence. Dialing her number it rung a few times before she answered. Telling her to come outside, I hung up and waited. Few minutes later shorty came strolling out the house, so I flicked my headlights letting her know where I was at.

"Hey," she spoke softly blushing.

"Sup with you?"

"Nothing. You okay?"

"I'm cool."

"Is that the truth?"

"Nah.. I'm not actually. Just got a lot of shit on my mental." I replied.

"What's wrong?"

"Life. A bunch of bullshit. Nothing in particular."

"Life happens to everyone Jensen. As far as the bullshit goes, we can't escape that baby." She spoke and never in my life have I heard my name mentioned like that.

"I know. I just be thinking about shit, and it just starts getting annoying. Like these are the cards life dealt to me."

"What do you mean?"

"All my life, life has been a struggle. I'm good now for the most part, but I ain't always have shit easy. I'm a black man in America with a fuckin' record. That shit travels with me everywhere. I think about where would I be if I was dealt a different hand but I come up short every time. My mind goes blank." I told her.

"You're thinking too much." she giggled grabbing my hand.

"Your fingernails are disgusting. Do you know that?"

"I don't pay attention to that. I wash my hands and shit. That's all that matters, right?"

"No, germs still live under your fingernails. You bite your nails, huh?"

"Yeah, it's a habit."

"That's a nasty habit to have. You have anxiety?"

"Ayo, wassup with all the questions?" I asked her chuckling.

"Nothing. I'm just being nosey." She giggled.

"What you study in school because you nosey as fuck."

"Psychology."

"I figured."

"That obvious huh?"

"Yeah with all the questions you've been asking. Observing behaviors in me and shit. Yeah, it was a dead giveaway. What made you decide on that?" I asked her out of curiosity.

"I used to people watch as a child. While other kids were out playing with toys and their friends. I would find me a spot secluded from everyone and watch people from a distance. I always wondered what they were thinking when doing certain activities or what could cause someone to go the hell off. It all intrigued me, so I wanted to study the human mind. I'm naturally an observer."

"I see."

"You ever think about going to school?"

"Nah. School ain't for me."

"How do you know if you never tried?"

"Trust me I just know," I told her checking the time.

"I gotta take care of some business. You going home tonight?"

"I don't know. Is there a reason I should be going home?"

"I wanna see you later."

"Later? Like what time?"

"I got some shit to do, but I should be back before the sun comes up."

"Where are you-" she started to ask before stopping.

"I don't want to know. If you're about to do something you have no business doing, I don't want to know anything. Just be safe."

"Always. So back to what I was saying. You going to let me come over or nah?"

"I guess. I'll leave a spare key under the mat."

"Aight, Ima see you later," I told her as she sat there pouting like she wanted to say something, but she didn't. Chewing on her bottom lip, she grabbed the door handle while I grabbed her arm closest to me.

"Don't worry. I'm good."

"Okay." She said just above a whisper as her voice cracked getting out the car. Before she closed the door, she stuck her head in kissing me quickly.

"Be safe Jensen."

"I will. No worries." I told her and pulled off.

Here goes nothing.

Skylen

"Where did you disappear to?"

"Went outside for a few," I responded picking up my drink.

"Okay." My mother responded messing with her mail.

"Mom, how did you cope? You know after daddy died."

"Well, I had you and your brother to look after so I had no choice but to keep moving. If it weren't for the two of you, I probably would have let my grieving and depression swallow me whole. Having a hard time?"

"Yes. I know he's gone, but a part of me still doesn't want to accept it. Like I know he isn't coming back, but I still keep thinking he's going to pop back up."

"Oh honey, you're going to go through that for a

while. You just have to stay strong. It isn't going to be easy, but you have to fight to get better. Leland wouldn't want you torturing yourself like this."

"I know, but I can't help it. I've been managing but some days are truly harder than others. I have Lauren, you and this guy friend of mine but I still find that other days I'm simply forcing myself to be okay." I explained before my mind started replaying random memories of Leland and I. Some good. Some bad. They were memories though nonetheless.

***

I had just gotten in from work. We had spent the whole weekend moving into our own place and between work and that I was tired. I could pass out right where I stood, but instead, I dragged myself to the bedroom where Leland layed in the bed sound asleep like he had no care in the world.

Taking my clothes off, I slid under the covers getting comfortable. That's just how tired I was. I never get into bed without showering first but seeing as though I work at a call center and knowing that if I even attempted to shower, I would probably fall and bust my ass in the shower.

Turning over to my side, I closed my eyes and said a brief prayer to myself. I prayed that God blessed my friends and family. I prayed that Leland would find a freaking job. I was the only breadwinner at the moment, but I was hoping that wouldn't last long. It was starting to get to me.

I've been cool this far, but I feel like all my money goes into providing for the both of us. Not to mention I only work part-time but I'm starting to think I may have to go full time. I wasn't trying to be stuck at this job for long though. I wanted to find a job in Psychology seeing as though I recently got my degree.

Pulling the covers up to my neck he wrapped his arms around me from the back, and I rolled my eyes. He wanted some pussy, but I wasn't in the mood to give him any. He didn't deserve any. At least, in my opinion, he didn't. Taking one of his hands he tried pinching one of my nipples and I slapped his hand away.

"Stop Le."

"Come on beautiful, my dick is hard."

"So? What that mean?" I asked with an attitude while he still tried pinching my nipple.

"*You really ain't gon' take care of ya man? That's what you tellin' me?*"

"*Leland, I am tired. I've been working all night, and the last thing I'm thinking about is poppin' my coochie.*"

"*You don't even have to do anything. Just lay there. I'll do all the work.*" *He tried to bargain, but I still wasn't with it.*

I wasn't turned on a bit. He was humping my ass from the back and everything, but I just wasn't feeling it. If I gave him some he would have to spit start my pussy because ain't no way she juicing up for him. Sorry, not sorry.

"*Stopppp Le. Damn!*" *I spat gettin irritated.*

"*What part of I'm tired don't you understand. I just came in from work. You've slept all night. I haven't. I'm fuckin' tired.*"

"*You know what they say if you don't do it another woman will,*" *He said trying to get under my skin, but it didn't work. I simply closed my eyes before responding.*

"*Enjoy. Hopefully, she does it better than me.*"

"*I see you're just the comedian this morning.*"

"I'm just saying. If you cheat on me bitch, make sure she does everything better."

"If you would just give me some pussy we wouldn't even be talking about this right now." He grumbled getting out of bed.

"Awww boo boo cry. Don't be mad. Maybe I'll give you some later." I told him, but he didn't say anything.

He'll be alright. Maybe I'll give him some later. Just maybe.

***

He was so mad that day, he jumped out of bed and slept on the sofa for two days because I wouldn't give him any. He was mad at the fact that he had to use his hand, but I didn't care. If he would have let me get some rest I would have been fine, and just maybe I would have given him some, but he didn't so guess what? He never gotten any.

Can you believe after that day he continued to have an attitude and accuse me of cheating? He accused me of cheating. The girl who didn't lose her virginity until I was 21. I never stepped outside of our relationship. I never had the desire to which was why when I met Sen I was embarrassed for having a connection with him. I'm still not sure what drew me to him, but I couldn't help but gravitate towards him.

"Skylen you don't hear me talking to you?" My mother asked me taking me out of my thoughts.

"Sorry. I had spaced out for a second. What did you say?" I asked looking at her.

"Who is this guy friend?"

"His name is Jensen."

"Jensen? What woman names a child Jensen?"

"Mommy!"

"What? I'm just asking a question. You don't think that's an odd name? Jensen. Sounds like something that goes into tea." She said with her nose turned up.

"Not tea momma!" I said giggling.

"So what's the story with you and this Jensen

character?"

"Nothing. We're friends."

"Sky."

"Mom, trust me we're just friends."

"You know a lot of people think it's cool to jump into another relationship after a breakup. Technically you and Leland didn't breakup-" she started saying, and I had to tell her the truth.

"Ma, Leland and I was broken up when he.. when he.. you know." I sighed.

"It wasn't working so I left. I kicked him out and shortly after he was killed." I continued to say trying to hold back tears.

"Baby. I didn't. I didn't know."

"I just feel like it's all my fault! I should have never kicked him out. He would still be here!"

"Sky. Baby." She spoke getting up and sitting next to me.

"Nothing you would have done would have

prevented this from happening. It's not your fault, and you shouldn't blame yourself. You hear me? You can't blame yourself because some coward did what he did."

"It hurts momma. It hurts." I cried laying my head on her shoulder.

Valencia

"This is the house," I told Sen when he pulled up to this ranch style house.

"You sure?" he asked looking at me.

"Positive. This is the address he had given me before."

"So how we doing this again?"

"You stay out here, and I'll go in the house."

"V. That's mad risky. I ain't bouta let you do that shit."

"Sen. Trust me. I'll be quick, nobody is here. I'll be in and out. Trust me. Okay?"

"Mannnn."

"Trust me Sen!"

"Aight man. If you ain't out here in ten minutes, fifteen tops I'm coming in. Aight?" He question and I nodded my head before getting out of the car and walking around to the side door.

I remember when I stayed the night with him, he said something about the lock on the door wasn't on correctly. Taking out a bobby pin I had, I stuck it in the keyhole and messed with it for a while before I heard the door unlock. Making sure not to make too much noise I turned the flashlight on my iPhone on and navigated my way to his bedroom.

Tee was stupid. He kept his money in a shoebox in the closet. Typical hiding spot for a hood nigga. I saw him go in it when he thought I was asleep. Unfortunately for him I was three steps ahead just in case he switched up and he did. Moving boxes out of the way, I got to the box to the very back that was taped up. Grabbing it, I opened it, and there was the money. Putting everything back as best as I could I walked back through the house and left out the same way I had came in.

"Finished?" Sen asked me when I got into the car.

"Yup. I told you it would be quick and easy." I told him, and he pulled off. Opening the box fully it was filled with bankrolls. Guess the nigga was really making moves. I thought his ass was bluffing. You know niggas be acting like they're the head nigga in charge but really be the runner? I thought that was him.

"Sen."

"Sup?"

"Thank you."

"Thank you? For what?"

"For everything. For opening my eyes. Thank you."

"You aight?" He asked chuckling.

"Of course, silly. I can't tell you thank you?" I asked turning in my seat to look at him as he drove.

"You can do whatever it is that you want to do. It's your world baby girl. I'm just living in it." He said just as his phone rang. Pulling it out he glanced at it before silencing it.

"Who's that?"

"Nobody."

"Was that her?" I asked nervously.

"Her? Who is her?"

"The girl you're seeing. Was that her?"

"I don't know what you're talking bout V."

"Sen. You don't have to lie to me. We haven't been intimate in a while. You're rarely home. I know it's another woman."

"You know, you shouldn't ask questions that you don't want to know the answers to." He stated in a serious tone never looking at me.

"I know there's somebody else in the picture. I'm not stupid."

"Then the fuck you asking questions for if you know the truth already?"

"I didn't ask to start a fight but let's face it. Our relationship has been over for a while. You checked out a long time ago, and I need to accept that."

"Yeah? And when did I check out? When you came home with dick on your breath?"

"I deserve that," I said to him shutting up.

Sen and I was done. I wanted to repatch things at one point but now I just wanted to move forward with my life. After we got home, I was leaving and never looking back.

Sen

Taking my hands, I slid them over my face as I sat in the car outside V and I crib. She had gotten out a few minutes ago, but I remained in the car. I was on the fence about going inside and crashing or just going to Sky's place. It was a little after two in the morning, and I didn't want to disturb her if she was asleep.

Finally getting out the car I made my way inside the house and to our bedroom. For a minute I stood there looking at Valencia as she undressed. The sight of her still made my man's stand up at attention, and since I wouldn't be sliding into Sky tonight, I guess Valencia will do.

"Come here," I demanded.

"Huh?"

"Come here."

"Sen, what you want?" She asked, but she knew to walk her ass over to me.

The second she was in front of me, I pushed her

against the wall and kissed her on her neck as I brought my hands down to her thongs and ripped them off her. Following my lead, she unbuckled my jeans and began pulling them down with the boxers I was wearing.

Picking her up, she wrapped her legs around my waist as I rammed my dick up in her roughly. Her eyes rolled to the back of her head as she enjoyed the strokes I was giving her. She liked this rough shit. I knew because her pussy was leaking something serious.

"Oooooh fuckkkkkkk!" She whimpered as my dick drilled at her opening.

"Sen, fuck your pussy!" She yelled.

"Yesssss, just like that. Just like that! Fuck meeeeeee."

"You's a nasty bitch huh?" I asked never slowing down.

With my dick still planted inside of her I walked her over to the bed we shared before removing myself from inside of her and flipping over. Arching her back perfectly I grabbed a hold to her hips and pushed my way inside slowly. Reaching one of my hands around to the front of her neck I choked her while my dick was still buried deep inside of her.

"Fuuuucckkkkkkkk!" She moaned fucking me back.

Every time she threw that ass back my dick disappeared. Valencia took my dick like a champ. I was giving her all nine inches, fucking her like I hated her. Unlike the other times, we've had sex this time was different. I didn't feel any emotions as I fucked her.

I felt her muscles contract around my dick, and I knew her cumming was only seconds away. Speeding up my strokes, her moans got louder.

"I'm about to cummmmmm!" She cried and just like she had said seconds before she came all over my dick.

Pulling out I walked into the bathroom and hopped in the shower. The moment she told me to fuck my pussy, my dick went soft a bit. I fucked shorty with a floppy, and she didn't even notice.

***

"Valencia?" I called out to her as I walked around the house but she never responded.

"Ayo V, where you at?" I called out again. Still nothing but silence.

Taking a seat on the sofa, I thought about where she could have gone. When I fell asleep, she was here, laying next to me so her not being here was kinda trippy. Spotting a folded piece of paper, I saw my name written on it. Picking it up, I opened it, and it was a letter from her.

Sen, I just want to say thank you for everything you have done for me. Thank you for being the best man you could possibly be for me. I know you woke up to find me not lying next to you, but this was the only way I could do this. I don't deserve you. I never deserved you. I need to go find myself and learn how to love myself before I can expect someone else to. Don't call looking for me, I'm okay. I just want you to be happy. You're more than this shit we've been doing. Open a business or something. Maybe one day we'll meet again. Maybe we won't who knows. If we never cross paths again, I want you to know that despite my infidelities, you were it for me. I just wasn't ready for you, but there's someone out there who is. Who knows, it just might the girl from last night but it isn't me. Be happy baby. Find your happiness.

Love Always V

I didn't see this coming. A nigga got left via a fucking love letter. How the fuck did that happen?

Skylen

Three Months Later

"Lauren can you hurry up!" I yelled at her as I stood outside her apartment drinking a bottled of water.

"Bitch hold ya horses!" She yelled back sticking her head out of the window.

"Wassup beautiful?" I heard a voice say and I turned around and smiled.

"Hey, Sen."

Sen and I was still kicking it. We weren't an item or nothing like that, but I enjoyed his company. I was still sleeping with him, however, but we never really talked about us. We just let things flow, and I preferred it that way.

"Miss me?" I asked him smiling.

"What you think?"

"I think you miss me. You stalking a bitch and shit."

"Stalking you? That's what you think?" He questioned licking his lips.

"I mean why else would you be poppin up to where I was at?"

"I was simply riding by."

"That's the lie you're going with?" I asked him wrapping my arms around his neck and kissing him softly on the lips.

"It ain't a lie if I'm telling the truth."

"I suppose."

"What y'all finna do?" he asked placing his hands on my booty. Thanks to him my ass was looking a little fatter these days. See what good dick will do to you?

"Shopping. Getting rid of all of my old things and buying new stuff for the new place."

"Nervous?"

"For?"

"Moving. A fresh start in another place."

"Kinda but I need it," I spoke to him still smiling.

Ever since Leland's death, I haven't been able to sleep. I tried to but I couldn't, so I went to see a therapist. Funny because I went to school for Psychology, but I paid a stranger to tell me that moving was the best option in order for me to start healing. I understood and agreed with her, so I did what I had to.

As I stood there with my arms wrapped around Sen's neck basking in the moment, his phone rang. Pulling it out of his pocket he answered it. Every other word he licked his lips driving me crazy. He knew I loved when he did that shit.

"I'm over here in I.O on Montgomery. Nah I should be here for a few. Where you at?.. Oh, word?.. Aight see you in a few." He said disconnecting the call returning his attention to me.

"Grimey."

"I didn't even ask." I giggled.

"You didn't have to. Your nosey ass was staring in my mouth the whole time."

"I am not nosey."

"Sky, you nosey as fuck. You know you are. Every time a nigga phone goes off you break your neck tryna see some shit."

"I do not," I replied still smiling.

"Police looking for somebody. Y'all don't hear them fuckin' sirens?" Lauren said finally coming outside just as four squad cars pulled up barricading us in.

"What the fuck is-" I started to say just as a police

officer yelled telling us to freeze and to put our hands in the air.

As they ran up on us, I looked at Sen, and his face held no emotion. A few moments ago, he was smiling and laughing with me, but now he was biting down on his back teeth.

"Jensen Lewis? You are under arrest for the murder of Leland Jacobs. You have the right to remain silent. Anything you." The officer read him his rights, and everything was a blur.

Did I just hear what I think I just heard? Sen, killed Leland? No that has to be a mistake. Right?

"Sen. Please. Tell me it's not true right? You didn't kill my. You didn't!" I yelled, and he just put his head down as they finished cuffin' him.

"Sky! Sky!" I heard Lauren yell, but I couldn't respond. I was feeling light headed, and before I knew it, everything went black.

Sen

Grimey had set a nigga up. Had I known this shit would have ended like this for me I would have never done it. I just want to know how the fuck did they even have enough evidence to lock me up. I left no traces of myself anywhere near the crime scene. I was careful, or so I thought.

Shit was probably bullshit. I might be able to get myself out of this. I had enough bread to find a good paying lawyer to fight this shit. What I couldn't do was unsee the look on Skylen's face when they were putting me in handcuffs.

I had no idea the nigga I went to murk was the nigga she was dating. I didn't even bother to put two and two together. I was thinking I was doing a favor for my nigga. You know? Looking out for him while getting some bread doing it.

The look on her face when his name left the officer lips will be a look I'll never forget. That shit fucked with me. It was like life as she has known it was over. Her heart was broken for a second time because of me and there was no way I could even take any of this back.

I fucked up. I didn't mean to, but I did. I liked baby something serious but wasn't no way I could bounce back from this shit. I was the cause of all the pain she was feeling. In her eyes, it probably looked like I was playing her all along but that wasn't the case. I gave a fuck about her and hopefully one day she could forgive me.

Damn who would've thought shit would have ended like this for us? We were just getting started. I had taken a life away from her and now mine was being taken away from me. Crazy how shit plays out, huh? Whole time I thought I was doing bro a favor, the muthafucka was ratting' me out.

Epilogue

Skylen

Seven Months Later

"You have a collect call from Sen-" the operator said, and I hung up.

It had been seven months since he was arrested for killing Leland and I hadn't spoken to him since the day they took him away. I felt played. I felt like he preyed on me just to fuckin hurt me. I wanted to know so bad why he did what he did but I don't even think it mattered at this point anymore. He did what he did, and it couldn't be undone.

I don't even know if I will ever forgive him for his betrayal. What I do know is I was all set on men for a while. Clearly the men I chose just weren't for me, or I was just fucking retarded.

Rubbing my stomach my heart ached. I was nine

months pregnant getting ready to pop any day now. The baby belonged to Sen. I found out I was pregnant the same day they arrested him. So much was going on that I ended up fainting and was transported to the hospital where it was revealed that I was pregnant.

At first, I was angry, but this child was innocent and was meant to be here. It wasn't his or her fault that their father was a fuck nigga. He knew I was pregnant. I kept in touch with his mother, so I'm sure she told him which was why he called me every single day in hopes that I would answer. I hadn't so far, and I had no desire to ever. Standing up I felt something wet rush down my leg.

"Just great, I peed on myself." I said in a frustrated tone waddling out of the bedroom and into Lauren's bedroom.

"Can you help me change? I peed on myself!"

"Sky.. You are too old to be pissin on-"

"Owwww!"

"Sky you're water broke bitch! Oh shit! Let's get

you to the hospital!" She said excitedly jumping up from her bed.

"Lauren.., this.. owwww," I said in pain.

Isn't it ironic how I talk about the damn man and this happens? This baby is about to be something else. I can already tell, but I was ready for all that came my way on this new journey I was about to embark on. Unfortunately, I didn't get the happy ending I always thought I would get. I imagined my life to be totally different, but life has a sense of humor, throwing you curve balls along the way leaving you to just deal with it.

Oh well, here goes nothing.

The End... Or is it?

SHE GOT IT BAD FOR A SPRINGFIELD HITTA